THINK RATHER
OF
ZEBRA

Dealing with Aspects of Poverty Through Story

Stories
adapted by

Jay Stailey

Introduction
and
Questions by

**Dr. Ruby
Payne**

Stailey, Jay C., & Payne, Ruby K.
   Think Rather of Zebra
Copyright © 1998 by **aha!** Process, Inc., xiii, 347 pp.
Illustrated by Robert W. Stailey; graphic design by
   Leigh Anne Marx and Toni McAfoos
Bibliography pp. 339-343
ISBN 0-9647437-5-2

1. Folktales   2. Sociology   3. Title

For information on storytelling and storyteller Jay Stailey, you may
contact him through **aha!** Process, Inc. at (800) 424-9484,
www.ahaprocess.com, or at his website, www.islandstories.com.

To the children at
G.W. Carver Elementary School:
We had hoped our generation would win the war
on poverty ...
Perhaps your generation can wage a war on greed.

INTRODUCTION

Dear Reader,

While working as principal at George Washington Carver Elementary School in Baytown, Texas (population: 65,000), I met Dr. Ruby Payne, then the director of staff development at Goose Creek School District. Every time I saw a central office administrator, I asked the question, "What about *these* kids?" "These kids" I referred to were the 900-plus children at Carver whose demographics looked peculiarly different from most students and schools in the district. The Carver kids were more than 90 percent minority and more than 90 percent poor (based on percentage of students who qualified for the federal lunch program). Nearly a third of the students at Carver were taught in a language other than English. In the beginning, more than half the students were unable to meet minimum mastery on the Texas Assessment of Academic Skills (TAAS) test.

In short, despite special programs and nationally recognized innovative initiatives (Chapter I schoolwide project, bilingual program, HOSTS tutoring, Saturday morning sessions, parenting programs, early-childhood intervention, dual-language multi-age), we were much like similar schools in the nation whose halls were filled with low-income students. We were yet another middle-class institution with a miserable track record when dealing with the students and parents from the culture of poverty.

In Ruby Payne, I encountered an educator who had spent many years contemplating the question, "What about these kids?" While working with the students and staff at Carver and other schools in the district, Dr. Payne was able to put twenty years of observation and thought together and write the book Poverty: A Framework for Understanding and Working with Students and Adults from Poverty. As she began to make presentations in Texas, and eventually on the national level, our conversations and discussions continued. Her work included a close look at the oral tradition within the culture of poverty and the place and structure of story within that culture. During one of our conversations, Dr. Payne pointed out a need for a collection of stories to be used to illustrate and reinforce the points she was making in her presentations.

After a short pause, Dr. Payne looked at me and said, "I believe you know those stories." She was very persuasive. For more than a year, she met with me, talked with me, and encouraged me, setting and resetting deadlines. "I work much better under deadlines," she told me.

With the help of many people in the storytelling community—especially Houston tellers Jeannine Pasini-Beekman and Sally Goodroe, Texas tellers Elizabeth Ellis and Tom McDermott, and "alien" tellers Chris Maier and Sunwolf—I was able to gather and write these stories. With the editing and production assistance of Paula Fornfeist, Dan Shenk, and Toni McAfoos, and the artwork of Leigh Anne Marx, along with my father, Bob "The Zebra Man" Stailey, I am able to present the stories in this format.

I want to thank everyone who had the patience to watch me work and to wait, especially my family. I hope this presentation of stories can be useful in the struggle to help middle-class institutions work successfully with those who come from the culture of poverty.

WARNING! Many of these stories have made appearances in books and other places and have been told by gifted storytellers in the recent past. I have gathered the tales together here to enlighten a specific path toward understanding. My apologies go out to those who have told these stories elsewhere and in many ways have given unique life to these traditional tales. I have tried to give you, the reader, specific story reference points in the Epilogue of this book.

The power of story is greatly underestimated. May these stories be used to teach, to enlighten, and to build bridges of human connection.

Jay Stailey

Dear Reader,

When Jay Stailey and I first started talking about this book, he was president of the National Storytelling Association and principal at G.W. Carver Elementary School, which was the school in Baytown, Texas, with the highest percentage of poverty. Both of us were struck by how much of the important information in poverty that gets conveyed orally is done so through story.

As I began to travel and do workshops on poverty, many people asked how we can teach the hidden rules, the basic understandings that an individual needs to know in order to be successful in the world of school and work. I suggested that "story" would be the natural vehicle.

This book is meant to be a tool for discussion and teaching. Stories can be told, read aloud, or read silently. The responses are meant to be given orally, though a written learning log could be kept. You may wish to develop further questions. Many of these stories lend themselves to a variety of learning opportunities.

Jay's stories touched my heart. It is only as we work together, each in our own way, that we will begin to address the issues of poverty.

Joe Jaworski, in his book Synchronicity, states, "If individuals and organizations operate from the generative orientation, from possibility rather than resignation, we can create the future into which we are living, as opposed to merely reacting to it when we get there."

The questions I've developed to go with Jay's stories are dedicated to the possible.

Ruby Payne

TABLE OF CONTENTS

INTRODUCTION v

TABLE OF CONTENTS x

PROLOGUE: Think Rather of Zebra: Dealing
with Aspects of Poverty Through Story .. 1

CHAPTER 1
Tales of Poverty and Wealth 2
    The Remarkable Dreams of Rufus Burns 3
    The Millionaire 7
    Miss Thornton's Poor Sister 10
    Willie, the Shoeshine Man 13
    QUESTIONS: CHAPTER 1 20

CHAPTER 2
The Role of Language and Story 23
    The Argument in Signs 25
    The Barn Is Burning 30
    The Family Tradition 36
    QUESTIONS: CHAPTER 2 38

CHAPTER 3
Referring to Resources 41
    Secret Number One: Mental Resources 42
      Common Sense 42
    Secret Number Two: Financial Resources 47
      A Dozen Kernels of Corn 49

Secret Number Three: Emotional Resources 54
  One Whisker from the Wild Dog 55
  The Single Flame (Part 1) 60
Secret Number Four: Role Models 63
  The Single Flame (Part 2) 63
  Getting Out of a Load of Trouble 67
Secret Number Five: Support Systems 70
  Spread Your Fingers When You Eat 71
Secret Number Six: Spiritual Resources 75
  The Bleacher Bum 76
Secret Number Seven: Physical Resources 80
  Carlos and the Flying Boat 82
  QUESTIONS: CHAPTER 3 102

CHAPTER 4
Hidden Rules Among Classes 109
  Cousin Jimmy's Dilemma 112
  An Experiment in Distance Learning 118
  The Alley Cat's Secretary of State 122
  A Vest Pocket Full of Beef 130
  QUESTIONS: CHAPTER 4 135

CHAPTER 5
Spring Break: A Leisurely Look at the
Characteristics of Generational Poverty ... 139
  The Woman in the Blue House on Oak Street ... 140
  Little Eight John 147
  The Eagle Chick 153
  In Whose Hands Is the Fate of the Army? 157
  The Story of Coach 'Stump' Barnes 160
  Looking for Paradise 166
  A Bird in the Hand 171
  QUESTIONS: CHAPTER 5 176

CHAPTER 6

**Role Models, Emotional Resources,
and Decision-Making** 181

    A Million Ideas 182

    Strength 188

    Joey Brings Home His Pay 196

    The Best Thief 204

    The Gardener's Son's Quest 214

    QUESTIONS: CHAPTER 6 230

CHAPTER 7

Support Systems: Use and Abuse 235

    The Seven Sisters' Situation 236

    Cricket Harrison's Reputation 242

    Cricket Harrison Settles a Wager 249

    A Matter Between Friends 255

    QUESTIONS: CHAPTER 7 264

CHAPTER 8

Discipline: Choices and Consequences 266

    The Crane Wife 267

    The Gardener's Choice 277

    Not Our Problem 282

    Fear 286

    Anger 287

    Confusion 289

    QUESTIONS: CHAPTER 8 293

CHAPTER 9

About Instruction: Knowing and Learning .. 296

Uncle Kenneth's Axe Handle 297

The Sky Is Falling 302

The Blind Dixie Gospel Quartet Meets the

King of the Circus 306

Turtle Learns to Fly 310

Wisdom or Air? 313

Joey Meets the Board of Education 317

QUESTIONS: CHAPTER 9 320

EPILOGUE

Story Roots 325

The Perfect Shot 325

ROOTS OF THE STORIES 328

RESOURCES 339

ABOUT THE AUTHOR 345

PROLOGUE

A student had studied for a long time and felt that he was finally ready to leave his teacher.

"You are not ready," the teacher told him with a gentle smile.

"Why not?" asked the student, almost indignantly.

"You have not yet learned the meaning of story," replied the teacher.

The student looked so disappointed that his teacher added quietly, "Stories can teach us a new way of seeing things, of thinking about them, and of responding."

Because he could see that his student still did not understand, the wise teacher reached out to help once again. "When you hear hoofbeats, what do you think of?" he questioned in a soft voice.

"Why, a horse, certainly!" answered the student with confidence.

"That is because you have become conditioned, and in that conditioning you have fallen asleep," the patient teacher pointed out. "When you hear hoofbeats—think rather of zebra."

In the eye of the student a glimmer of understanding shone. Turning to the teacher, he said, "Tell me a story."

CHAPTER 1

Tales of Poverty and Wealth

In a tired neighborhood, in an old brick housing project, ten-year-old Carlos lives with his mama. Though outsiders might be afraid to travel in these streets, this is Carlos' neighborhood, and these are Carlos' streets (truth be told, fear is a large part of Carlos' life). On a steamy, late-summer afternoon, he sat on some steps and conversed with Pete about being rich one day. Carlos knew that Pete, an older man with a patch on one eye, could see more with his good eye than most of the rest of the neighborhood combined (except for Carlos' mama). Pete smiled at Carlos and asked, "Did I ever tell you about how Rufus Burns got himself rich?" Pete leaned back and took a breath, then off he went ...

The Remarkable Dreams
of Rufus Burns

Rufus was a street peddler who lived over on First Avenue. He had a little house in front of his stable. I believe his horse Maybelle had more room in the stable than Rufus had in his house. I know that the yard in between was barely big enough for a little cherry tree. This all happened before the city government and the Sac 'n Save put street peddlers like Rufus out of business. Early in the morning, way before the sun came up, Rufus would hitch up his wagon to Maybelle and go down to the farmers' market and buy fruits and vegetables. By mid-morning, you could hear the clip-clop of Maybelle's hooves and the chanting song that Rufus would sing out about the produce on his wagon. He would sell apples and bananas and peaches and plums to the folks on their way to work, or maybe a snack, an apricot or grapes, to those already working. For the folks still at home, his song would roust them out and get them moving to the tune of "Tomaaaatoes, ohhhkra, fresh-picked collard greens." He didn't

3

get rich pulling his wagon and singing his song, but he survived. Some days, Mister Rufus even sold some of the ripe cherries off that little tree in his yard. I bet even your mama remembers eating some of Mister Rufus' ripe cherries.

"You know that's right," Carlos said, kicking at an ant on the sidewalk. "But how'd he get rich?"

Back one spring, Rufus woke up earlier than early and shook his head. It wasn't time to get up, but he couldn't sleep because he'd had a dream. He dreamed if he went into Houston to City Hall down on Bagby Street and stood on the front steps, he would discover an amazing thing. But time was moving, and he didn't want to take time worrying about foolish dreams. So he got up, hitched Maybelle to the wagon, and went on over to the farmers' market. By the time the sun was up, he was so busy greeting his neighbors with his fruit-and-vegetable chant, he didn't think any more about that dream. Problem was, the next night he had that same dream again. And the next night.

"Same dream, huh?" Carlos was trying not to be interested.

You got that right. And after he had that same dream three nights running, well, you know what they say about dreams like that. He skipped the farmers' market altogether and got a ride into Houston. From mid-morning to late in the afternoon, Rufus stood on those City Hall steps waiting to discover something amazing. But the only thing even a little bit amazing that he discovered was how hot those steps were and how loud his stomach complained about being ignored. He finally went over and sat on a bench under the big oak trees at the library building. No one is real sure where he spent the night that night, but the next morning he was back on the City Hall steps hoping to discover something amazing. The fact that he didn't give up and come home was the only amazing thing about that day. He stayed right downtown, and the next morning, that crazy Rufus was out there on those steps again. Late in

the afternoon of that third day, a policeman got to wondering whether he should give Rufus a ticket for loitering or just run him off. In order to decide, the officer asked Rufus what he was doing there, and Rufus told him about his dreams. That officer looked at Rufus as if he was plum out of his mind and then busted out laughing.

"You old fool," the cop said. "Certainly you got better things to do than spend three days chasing some ignorant dream. Why, if I spent my time chasing stupid dreams, I wouldn't be walking my beat right now. I'd be off in some tired old neighborhood east of Houston, trying to find me a peddler's yard with a cherry tree in it. Because I had a dream just last night that if I found that tree and dug at its roots, I'd find where some bank robbers hid a bag full of money."

Old Rufus, he recognized an amazing discovery when he heard one, and that policeman didn't even have to invite him to leave. He came home that very evening, slept all night without dreaming once, and the next morning he dug under that cherry tree and found a bag of money. That's how Mister Rufus got rich.

And do you know what?

6

"What?" Carlos asked, looking up at that gleam in Pete's one good eye.

There was no end to the good Mister Rufus did in this neighborhood after that amazing discovery. And that wasn't including his fruits and vegetables. I bet your mama remembers Mister Rufus. He was a good man.

The next morning, Pete noticed that Carlos was counting the pennies in his pocket. "If I had two more pennies," Carlos said, looking up at Pete, "I'd be all set when the ice cream man comes around." Pete replied, "Let's go find us a millionaire; maybe he can make up the difference."

The Millionaire

Carlos jumped down off the steps. He could not imagine where Pete was going to take him to find a millionaire. He thought maybe they would get a ride out to the Interstate. He had seen a rich guy on the TV who sold cars out on the Interstate. He also thought Pete might take him down by the new marina. Carlos had seen big boats down there and a new restaurant they were building ... and imagined it must take a million dollars to own a big motorboat or build a new restaurant. But Pete didn't even walk toward his old car. He was heading up Carver Street toward the clinic. Carlos was wondering where Pete was going to find a millionaire up by the clinic. Before they got to the clinic, they turned on Willow and ended up standing on the sidewalk in front of the barber shop. It was all the usual bunch, men his mama had warned him about hanging around—some teenagers, and some a little older, plus a few old men like Buddy Jacks, a blues guitar man. "Well, here's your man." Pete nodded toward Buddy Jacks and winked at Carlos. Carlos couldn't believe it. He knew Buddy Jacks. Sometimes, when Buddy had a few gigs, people claimed he was flush and tossed his money around like it was newspaper in the wind. Carlos also knew Buddy Jacks sometimes came around his grandma's house and was grateful that his grandma was a good cook and a gracious woman. Carlos knew if it weren't for his grandma, Buddy

Jacks would have gone hungry more than a few times. It was apparent on the days when Buddy came calling, he didn't have a dime to his name.

Just then the tune from the ice cream truck came wafting down Willow Street. Before Carlos could reach into his pocket and count his pennies, Buddy Jacks was holding two quarters out toward him. Carlos thanked him, grabbed the quarters, and ran down to the corner to catch the ice cream man. On the way back to his mama's house, Carlos told Pete about the times that Buddy Jacks had been so busted that Carlos' grandma had to feed him or he would've starved to death. Carlos fell silent, and Pete watched him lick on his popsicle. Carlos finally looked up.

"I see now that you wanted to meet someone who had a million dollars," said Pete with a smile. "I thought I'd show you better than that. I wanted to introduce you to someone who had *spent* a million dollars. In our neighborhood, that's a real millionaire!"

On Friday morning, Carlos turned the corner on MLK and ran smack into Pete. Pete was standing quite still, his hat in his hands, as he watched a funeral procession roll by. "Miss Thornton," he clarified quietly out of the corner of his mouth. Carlos stood erect until the line of cars following the hearse had gone over the railroad tracks, then he turned to Pete.

"Won't hear her complaining about being poor anymore. Think life is better where she's heading?"

Miss Thornton's Poor Sister

When Lily Thornton's sister May died, Pete started, settling down onto the steps, folks said she went straight to heaven. When she reached the pearly gates, she was standing next to a man who was obviously very rich.

St. Peter arrived and invited the rich man to enter at the pearly gates. Sister May peeked though the gates and watched as St. Peter and the rich man walked into the golden city.

What she saw really got her steamed! A chorus of angels greeted St. Peter and the rich man with a rousing trumpet fanfare, and people filled the streets shouting. When the noise died down, St. Peter gave a short but passionate speech and finished by saying, "Welcome to the City of God. Make yourself at home." As the rich man walked down the street, people began to shout and wave.

When the excitement had come to an end, St. Peter opened the gates, then bowed and beckoned for Miss May to enter. By now Miss May was really mad, and she decided to give St. Peter a piece of her mind.

"This is the last place I ever expected to be treated this way. I spent a lifetime on earth being discriminated against. All my days I watched rich people walk through doors that were slammed in the face of folks like me. I did not expect to face the same treatment on my first day in God's heavenly kingdom! I thought that here all people would at least be treated equally. But look ... now the crowds are all gone, and there is no one left to cheer for Miss May Thornton."

"My dear friend," St. Peter replied, "I can see how it looks like discrimination, but I must explain. Everything will be the same for the both of you from here to eternity. It's just that today is a special occasion. We receive poor folks up here every day, but we haven't had a rich man for nearly eight years!"

And that, Carlos my man, is the truth!

"I know that's right," Carlos replied.

"I can't wait until school starts up again," Carlos told Pete.

"Why is that?" Pete asked, curious that Carlos would be anxious for the end of summer vacation.

"I want to ask my teacher for a definition of 'poor.' At the house I keep hearing Mama and the neighbor ladies talking about 'welfare for poor people,' and 'housing for poor people,' and 'poor Miss Annie, her with no family left,' and 'those poor Rockets getting beat by thirty points,' and don't be 'poormouthin' my man' till I can't tell for sure what 'poor' is."

"I look forward to finding out what your teacher has to say. It seems to me," Pete added, "that 'poor' has more to do with how a person feels than how a person is."

Willie, the Shoeshine Man

A few years ago, a shoeshine man lived in that yellow house right over there on Yupon

Street. He didn't own the house; a landlord owned the house. Willie, the shoeshine man, just moved in one day without benefit of a lease—or electricity and water, for that matter. At the time, the chief of police used to wander through the town late at night in street clothes trying to discover things that might be going on. Lots of nights he came into our neighborhood because he had a hard time figuring out how poor people lived. They say that one night he was walking down Yupon Street when he noticed a light shining inside that yellow house and heard a rather happy tune being whistled. He went up to the door and knocked. A voice from inside invited him in. He opened the door and stepped inside the room. Willie, the shoeshine man, sat in the middle of the room on a wooden box, reading a paper by the light of a lantern.

"May I join you?" the chief asked. "It's beginning to rain a little outside."

Willie got up and offered the crate to the stranger. While the rain pattered on the roof, the two men began to talk.

"How do you manage to get by these days?" the chief asked, noting that the house was empty

14

except for the wooden box that he was now sitting on.

"I shine shoes," Willie replied.

"Where is your shoeshine shop?"

"I can't afford a shop. I take my shoeshine box—you're sitting on it there—to the sidewalk in front of the clinic, or the Sac 'n Save. Then I shine shoes for folks as they need it."

"You shine shoes on the sidewalk? Can you make enough money that way?"

Willie spoke up with both patience and pride: "Each day I make just enough money to buy food for that day."

"Just enough for one day? Aren't you afraid that one day you won't make enough, and then you'll go hungry?"

"I let God worry about the 'one day,' and He helps me take care of the 'today.'"

As the police chief headed home later that night he decided to put Willie's 'a day at a time' philosophy to the test. The next day, he issued an order to his men that the $50 street vendor license be strictly enforced and include shoeshine men.

That night, the chief returned to Yupon

Street to see if Willie might be whistling a different tune. But to his surprise, Willie was sitting in that little house, still whistling a happy tune.

"My friend," said the chief, "I heard the police were cracking down on street vendors today and wondered if you had been able to make enough to buy food."

"Oh," replied Willie, "I was pretty angry when I heard I wouldn't be able to shine shoes. But I knew that I got a right to make a living, and I'd have to find a way. As I stood on the corner telling myself that very thing, a group of people came up the sidewalk. When I asked them where they were headed, they told me they were going out on the highway to pick up aluminum cans. I asked if I could join them and they said, 'It's a big old highway. Come ahead.' So I picked up aluminum cans. At the end of the day I was able to sell them for just enough money to buy food for today."

"Just enough for today?" said the police chief with a hint of disgust in his voice. "What about tomorrow? What about next week?"

"I let God worry about the 'one day,' and He helps me take care of the 'today.'"

The next day the police chief told his men to enforce the law about no pedestrians on the highway. He told them that anyone caught walking out on the highway should be forced to join the National Guard and receive no pay for thirty days.

That night he returned to Yupon Street and, to his amazement, Willie, the shoeshine man, was still whistling a happy tune. There he sat on

the wooden box, whittling on a piece of wood. When the chief inquired about Willie's day, he got the whole story.

"The police caught me out by the highway picking up aluminum cans and made me join the National Guard. At the National Guard office, they issued me a uniform and gun, made me stand at attention all day, and said I wouldn't get paid for a month!"

"Oh, my friend, I bet you wish now that you had saved some money."

"Well, let me tell you what I did. At the end of the day, I looked at that gun and thought, *This baby's worth some money!* So on the way home, I took it to the pawn shop, got this whittling knife and just enough money to buy food for today. Now I'm whittling a gun out of this piece of wood that will look just like the one I pawned."

The police chief was stunned. "But what if one day you have to use that gun in the line of duty?"

"I let God worry about the 'one day,' and He helps me take care of the 'today.'"

The following day, while Willie, the shoeshine man, was standing post at the armory, the police chief sent some men to order him to guard a captured fugitive. "If he tries to escape," they grunted, "shoot to kill!"

"Shoot to kill? I'm not a soldier, I'm just a shoeshine man."

"If you don't shoot to kill, we'll figure you must be in with him."

Willie watched the man closely as a crowd began to gather. Slowly the man began to back into the crowd, looking out of the corners of his eyes for an escape route. Without hesitating, Willie shouted, "Let God be my witness: I am no murderer! If this man is guilty as charged, let my gun fire straight and true. But if he is innocent, let my gun turn to wood!"

He pulled his gun and aimed at the prisoner. But when the gun did not go off, he looked at it strangely, then dropped it on the pavement with a wooden *clunk*. The crowd gasped, and whispers of mystery turned to shouts of miracles.

At that moment the police chief came forward and identified himself to Willie as his night visitor. He invited Willie to move in with him at his house and be his advisor. I think he was still hoping to figure out how Willie could live so happily, one day at a time.

But Willie declined his offer and returned to that little house there on Yupon Street. He's gone now, Pete added, but as far as I can tell, every bit of that story is the truth.

QUESTIONS: CHAPTER 1
Tales of Poverty and Wealth

The Remarkable Dreams of Rufus Burns

1. What is poverty? What is wealth?

2. How did Rufus get rich?

3. Rufus followed his dreams. When you follow your dreams, do you always get rich? Is wealth about money?

4. Rufus gives back to his neighborhood. "There is no end to the good he did." Why is it important to give back?

5. What are your dreams for your life? What would you do if you have talent, money, happiness, success?

The Millionaire

1. Pete defines a millionaire as someone who "had spent a million dollars. In our neighborhood, that's a real millionaire!" In some groups of people, wealth is defined as how much money you save and invest. In some groups of people, it is defined by how much you spend. What is it in your neighborhood?

2. The middle class has a rule about money: "I don't ask you for money and you don't ask me." In Pete's neighborhood, money is shared. If you need money, you ask someone for it and it will be given. Do you share your money? If you have enough money, do you buy for everyone?

3. Some people use their money for entertainment, music, parties, and relationships. Others use their money to buy houses, cars, education, and consumer items. Still others use their money to purchase art, one-of-a-kind objects, and land holdings. What do the adults you know do with their money?

Miss Thornton's Poor Sister

1. Many people think having money is bad and being poor is to be closer to God. In the story, St. Peter comments on how long it has been since a rich person has been admitted to heaven. Is it bad to have money? Is it more difficult to get into heaven if you have money?

2. May Thornton is mad and says, "All my days I watched rich people walk through doors that were slammed in the face of folks like me." Are poor people discriminated against? Why or why not?

3. Pete suggests that, in the end, poor is only what you believe it is. Is that true? Why or why not? Give examples.

4. Can you be wealthy and not have much money?

Willie, the Shoeshine Man

1. Poverty is about survival. When all the chips are down and push comes to shove, the ability to survive is critical. Willie is a survivor. How does he do it?

2. Why won't Willie go live with the police chief?

3. Why is Willie happy, even though he has very few things?

4. There are eight resources that make a big difference in the success and survival of a person. These resources are: mental, emotional, physical, spiritual, financial, support systems, knowledge of hidden rules, and role models. Which of these resources does Willie have? Which resources do you have?

CHAPTER 2

The Role of Language and Story

One autumn afternoon, not so long after the school year began, Carlos rode his bike over to Pete's and sat on his step. Pete noticed that Carlos wasn't in one of his talkative moods.

"How's school going?"

"Okay," Carlos answered with a shrug, flipping a stone off the curb.

Pete let it set for a while, giving the silence some space on the second step. Finally, he asked, "What's the deal?"

"You know," Carlos started, "when my mama talks to me, I always understand what she's saying."

"Even when you'd like not to," Pete observed.

"You got that right! And when my grandma talks to me, even though she talks different than my

mama, I always understand what she's saying to me. When you tell me stories, I understand what you're saying, though sometimes it takes me a little while to figure out the stories."

"But you do figure them out."

"Right. But, at school, I have lots of problems trying to figure out what people are talking about. The principal comes on the loudspeaker in the morning and talks kind of high and mighty, almost like the preacher. Then he says the same thing again, only in Spanish. I swear, when the teacher is talking about percentages and decimals, she might as well be talking Greek. After school the older kids start flashing gang signs, and I don't have a clue what they mean either, and that really bothers me."

"I see what you mean. It leaves a lot of room for misunderstanding, doesn't it?"

Pete didn't expect an answer, and Carlos didn't give him one. It left a little space on the second step that Pete decided to fill up with a story.

The Argument in Signs

Way back, and not too far from here, there was a neighborhood just like this one. A group of neighbors had lived there a long time, and they liked to think they ran the place. They even had their own little government, and they chose a leader to make all the important decisions for the neighborhood. This worked pretty well for a while. But then some new folks began to move into the neighborhood, and the leader didn't like these new neighbors at all. In fact, he organized his friends and made life pretty miserable for the newcomers.

He finally decided it was time to take care of the problem once and for all. He put word out on the street he was going to offer up three signs. "If one of the newcomers can read my signs, then we won't give them any more trouble. But if they fail, we're going to run them out of town once and for all."

The new neighbors got together and tried to figure out what to do. Some said the plan was a trick, and they should leave town while it was still safe. Others looked for a leader among them who would face the challenge. Finally, an older woman stepped forward, offering to take on the task. She was a little bit of a thing who raised chickens in her backyard. Strangely enough, she had a patch over one eye just like me. Although her friends were not sure she was capable, they were glad she was at least willing to step forward and face their enemy and answer his signs.

The next morning, after the chicken lady did her chores, she scooped up her rooster and headed up the street to debate in signs. Seeing the little chicken lady come up the street with a patch over her eye and a rooster under one arm caused quite a bit of snickering among the large group of old-timers gathered on the Main Street corner.

Their leader stepped forward and began the debate by holding one finger up in front of him. The chicken lady stared silently for just a moment and then held up two fingers. The leader then reached into a pocket and brought out a piece of cheese. The chicken lady stuck her free hand into her pocket and held up an egg, which she had taken from a nest that morning. The leader then reached into his other pocket, pulled out some cornmeal, and threw it on the street between them. The chicken lady looked at the cornmeal, then set her rooster down on the street. The rooster pecked away, eating up the cornmeal, and then flew up and landed on the street sign above their heads.

The neighborhood leader shook his head in amazement. "She has answered each of my signs correctly," he announced. "She and her friends can stay right here, and we will give them no more trouble."

Later in the day, the leader's friends asked for an explanation and he informed them what had taken place. "I held up one finger to let her know there was only one law in this neighborhood, and that was my law. But she held two fingers up to remind me there was the law of God and the law of man. Then I took out a piece of old cheese to let her know we think that she and her friends are stinky and moldy. But she took out an egg to explain they are really warm and fresh. Finally, I threw down the cornmeal to show them we are powerful enough to throw them and all their possessions out into the street any time we wanted. She put down her chicken to let me know that they would gather up their belongings and keep coming back to roost right here in our neighborhood." The friends nodded soberly, clearly admiring the power of the old lady.

That same afternoon, the newcomers all gathered with their new heroine, the chicken lady, to find out how she had managed to answer all three signs correctly. "It was simple," she said. "First he held up one finger, making fun of the fact that I only have one eye and threatening to take it out. So I held up two fingers, letting him know if he threatened me again I would take out both of his eyes. Then he pulled out that old cheese, trying to make me feel hungry because he had food to eat and I didn't. So I let him know that I didn't need his stinky old cheese; I had fresh eggs every day. Finally, he acted like a fool, throwing that good cornmeal on the street. I didn't want it to go to waste, so I put my rooster down to have some breakfast."

"I know why you get frustrated at school," Pete said. "It's hard enough trying to understand the subjects. It's even harder sometimes understanding the school people. But that's what your mama sends you to school for. When you figure out what it is those folks are saying, then comes the hard part. You have to figure out what they mean."

Carlos thought about what he had just heard, and he understood exactly what Pete was saying. Carlos would just have to figure out what Pete meant later on. "What about the guys and the gang signs?" he asked.

"Well, now," Pete answered, "there are some ways of communication that just aren't worth the bother of learning. If I were you, I'd forget about the gang signs, and worry first about understanding the school talk."

The Barn Is Burning

Before I moved to the city, I worked out in the country near where my family was sharecropping. When I got old enough, maybe twelve years old, I got a job with the man at the head of the road who owned most of the farms in that area. I worked hard, in the fields for a while, and then up around the main house. When school started in the fall, that man told my parents I could live during the week up at his house to save me the long walk each morning to catch the school bus on the main road. In the fall, I stayed in a little room off the barn and ate with the hired hands. But when winter came, that man and his wife let me sleep in an attic room in the house, and I ate supper with them.

That man was a nice enough fellow. But he had a way of putting on airs and talking about things like he was the world's expert, when it was obvious he was just making most of it up as he went along. Almost every day his wife would ask me what I learned in school, and I could barely begin to tell her before he started some long speech about all the things he knew on the sub-

30

ject. So as the winter was ending, I was looking forward to moving back out into my little room in the barn.

One evening I came home from school, where the teacher had taught us how to say "hello" and "good morning" and "goodbye" in about five different languages. I had shown off my new knowledge to the lady of the house at the dinner table, and I could tell it  was bothering the old man that he couldn't keep up with me on that particular subject. After dinner, we were in the parlor room sitting around the fire, and he decided to show me what he knew.

"Pete," he said, pointing to the fire, "what is that?"

"Why, that's a fire, sir," I told him.

"No, it isn't," he responded. "That is a 'flame of evaporation.'"

Just then the cat passed in front of the fire, and the old man asked me, "Pete, do you know what that was that just passed in front of the fireplace?"

"That's the cat, sir," I answered.

"No, it's not either" the old man said. "That is a 'high-ball-a-sooner.'"

By that time I knew I was not going to answer any of his questions correctly, so I got up and went over to the window. I began staring out toward the barn, wishing winter was over. But the man got up from his chair and walked over to the window where I was. He pointed out to the haystack next to the barn. "Pete," he asked again, "what's that we are looking at through the window?"

"I'm looking at the haystack."

"That's not a haystack," he said with that tone of authority. "That is a 'high tower.'"

Well, that was enough of that nonsense for me. I sat down in the chair by the door and started untying the laces on my boots. I was ready to go upstairs to my attic room and did not want to track dirt on the carpet in the hallway. But that old man still was not finished with his impressive show of language. He pointed at my boots. "What are those?" he asked.

"Those are my boots."

"No, they aren't," he said. "Those are

'tramp-tramps.'"

When I stood up, and he saw that I was about to head upstairs, he pointed through the archway where I could see the bed in his bedroom. "What's that I am pointing to that is the same as what you are headed for in your attic room?"

"Why, that's a bed, sir," I said, knowing as soon as it came out of my mouth that it was certain to be the wrong answer.

"No, Pete," he replied, "that is a 'flowery bed of ease,' and I am headed right now to get into it. We are going to be up early in the morning with a long day ahead of us."

The old man and his wife went into their bedroom and went to bed. I went up the attic steps to my room and got ready for bed. Just before I climbed into my bed I did what I always did every school night: I got my homework, and my library book, and my school books. Then I put them by the door in the kitchen so I could pick them up on my way out in the morning to get the bus. As I started back up the stairs, I saw a flash in the corner of my eye. I looked over into the parlor room and saw the cat run too close to the fireplace and catch his tail on fire. That cat raised a howl and leaped out a window that the couple always cracked open even on the coldest night of winter. I watched through the window as that cat went streaking across the yard and over onto the haystack. The next thing I knew, the haystack was on fire.

I didn't waste any time. I immediately started shouting toward the master bedroom, "Sir! Sir! You better get up out of your flowery bed of ease and put on your tramp-tramps because your high-ball-a-sooner has run through the flame of evaporation and set your high tower to blazing."

The old man didn't move a muscle. He just chuckled to his wife and said, "Listen to Ol' Pete. He sure does have a knack for picking up those new languages."

The flames were getting higher, and now the barn was on fire so I shouted again, "Sir! Sir! You better get up out of your flowery bed of ease and put on your tramp-tramps because your high-ball-a-sooner has run through the flame of evapo-ration and set your high tower to blazing."

But the husband just chuckled to his wife again, "That sure is a clever boy we got living in the attic room. One day he may be as smart as I am."

I tried two or three more times to let him know what was happening, but he didn't move. Finally, when my little barn room caught on fire and I realized I might have to stay in the house when spring came, I shouted, "Mister, you better get yourself out of that bed and go out there and put out that haystack fire that your cat started, or else your whole darn farm is going to burn up!"

"I bet that got his attention pretty quick," Carlos said.

"Oh, it sure did. But by then it was too late to save the barn. When springtime came, I decided that I couldn't stand to listen to another word from that man. I quit school and went back up the road to help my daddy on his share."

Carlos looked up at Pete and saw that he was staring off as if, with that one eye, he could see back into the past and hope that he could change it. "That's a crazy story!" Carlos said under his breath.

35

Pete heard him. He turned and caught Carlos with one of his dark looks. "There is no such thing as a crazy story. Every story needs to be told. Every story needs to be heard. You never know what a story might do for you."

The Family Tradition

I knew a family once that went way back. They knew about stuff that happened to their family a hundred years ago. Back then, whenever there was a big problem (maybe something bad about to happen), the father would go off into the woods to a special place. When he found the place, he would light a fire in a special way, then say a special prayer for strength and patience. When he did this, the problem would not seem so big, and the family always made it through.

Years later, when the son and his family were facing bad times, he went off into the woods and found the place. He lit the fire in the special way, but he did not remember the words to the special prayer. Still, it was enough, and the family survived the hard times.

When the grandson was grown and had a family, he got into a ter-
rible situation. He went to the woods but could not find the special place. Still, he remembered how to light the fire, and he imag-ined his grandfather pray-  ing in the light of the flame. His family also man-aged to survive.

By the time the great-grandson came along, the family had moved to the city. When he was grown, and bad times landed in his neigh-borhood, he couldn't go to the woods. It was against the city ordinance to light fires inside the city limits, and he could not even imagine the words to that special prayer. But he knew the story, and just the story itself was enough to help his family face those bad times.

"Besides," Pete said to Carlos with a sly grin, "there is no better diversion in this life than a good story."

QUESTIONS: CHAPTER 2
The Role of Language and Story

The Argument in Signs

1. The chicken lady and the leader communicate without words: non-verbally. Some groups of people use non-verbal signals to communicate. If there has been a fight or near fight, and the reason given is "He was looking at me!" that is an example of using non-verbal "signs" to communicate. Do you know people who do that?

2. The chicken lady and the leader give different explanations about what the signs mean. Why?

3. Words are used to communicate, a way to share meaning, but sometimes people give different meanings to the same word. In addition, there are registers of language. Every language in the world has five registers. Two of these registers are formal and casual. Formal register is the language of the business community and educational community. Casual register is language used between friends and has broken sentences, general word choice, and many non-verbal signs. For example, in formal register a person would say, "School will be closed due to inclement weather." In casual register a person would say, "We ain't havin' school." Because formal register often uses twice as many words as casual register, it is difficult to understand formal register if you only know casual register. Formal register is used to teach in school and is taught in school. All tests are in formal register. Why does Pete say that it's hard sometimes understanding the school people? Describe the different registers of language used by the two participants in the "argument in signs."

4. How can formal register be learned?

The Barn Is Burning

1. Every group has special words to convey meaning. Some groups use words that have double meanings so that information can be in code. Some use special words so they know who is in their group and who is not. Do you know people who do this? Give examples. Can you also give historical examples?

2. Every group has stories that convey the important information and understandings about the way their group thinks and does things. Stories have structure and are told in different ways. In formal register, stories tend to go from the beginning to the end and have cause/effect, sequence, and focus on plot. In casual register, stories often start somewhere in the middle or close to the end. Stories are for entertainment, are episodic and random, include what is emotionally important to the teller, and focus on people. Can you give an example of each?

3. What stories do you hear from your friends?

4. What stories do you tell about yourself? There are different kinds of heroes: trickster hero, superman hero, antihero (e.g., Robin Hood), the caretaker, the fool. Can you think of different examples of stories about these hero types in your family or community?

The Family Tradition

1. How do stories help us?

2. What story or stories do you remember to help you through the bad times?

CHAPTER 3

Referring to Resources

Carlos watched the police arrest the brother of a classmate who lived up the street in the projects by the school.

"Makes a person wonder what's going to happen to him," Carlos said to no one in particular.

"Nothing's going to happen to you," Pete replied. "You're going to make it just fine."

"How do you figure?"

"I figure you have seven things that will get you by. Seven secrets. Seven tools in your tool chest. Yep, you're going to make it just fine."

"What seven secrets?"

SECRET NUMBER ONE:
MENTAL RESOURCES

You are a smart boy. Doesn't your mama brag about how good your grades are, even if you are kind of slow to get your homework done? Doesn't your teacher call on you in class? Aren't you always lugging a book around? That's one of the secrets. You have to be smart if you're going to make it.

Common Sense

On a sweltering hot summer day, a man lay in the shade of a tree wishing he could think of a way to get rich. He closed his eyes so as to think better, and before long he was hot and sweaty. He opened his eyes and squinted at the brightness of the sun. While he had been thinking, the sun had moved across the sky, the shade had moved across the earth, and he was no longer cool. So what do you think he did?

"Moved back into the shade?" Carlos suggested.

Right you are! It just made good sense. He got up and moved back into the shade. Then he closed his eyes again and tried to think of a way to get rich. Before long he was hot and sweaty. While he had been thinking the sun had moved across the sky, the shade had moved across the earth, and he was no longer cool. So what do you think he did this time?

"He got himself up and moved back into the shade."

Yep. Because it just made sense not to burn up out there in the sun. As soon as he went back into the shade, that's when he got his idea. If he could go around the neighborhood and collect all the common sense for himself, then, when people had a problem, they would have to come to him for advice. He could use the common sense, charge the people for his advice, and get rich. So, right that minute, he set out on his task. He found a big old bottle, made a stopper for the top, and went out looking for common sense.

Well, you know, everywhere he turned he found some. Things like "look both ways before you cross the street." He grabbed that up, stuffed it in the bottle, and put the stopper on. Things

43

like "go straight home after school," "don't ride your bike on the street after dark," "stay away from junior high boys." All those things that are just common sense, he snatched up and shoved into the bottle, then jammed the stopper back on. You know, things like ...

"Get your homework done before you go out to play?" Carlos suggested. "Don't hang around with strangers? Beware of girls!"

Yes, sir, all the common sense he could find in the world he stuffed into that bottle, until he had all there was, and the bottle was full. He was beginning to think of what he would do with all the money he was going to make selling advice, when he got nervous about that bottle. The common sense in that bottle was going to make him rich, and he surely didn't want anyone to steal it. He knew he needed to  find a good hiding place for it. He looked and looked, then finally decided to hide the bottle up in the tree he had been lying under when he got his idea.

So he would set up his advice business at the base of that shade tree. When people asked him for help, for the right price he would be willing to climb up the tree, find the perfect piece of common sense, bring it down, and share it with his customer. The only problem was ... he had to get that bottle of common sense safely up the tree. He found a piece of rope, tied the rope onto the neck of the bottle, then slung the rope around his neck. He rested that bottle right up against his fat stomach, so that it would be cushioned at all times. Then he grabbed hold of the tree and started to climb up.

On the first try that man got about half-way up the tree, but the bottle kept banging against the tree trunk and bouncing off his stomach. Finally, he lost his grip and slid down the tree. The man spit on his hands and rubbed them together. He repositioned the bottle safely against his stomach, and started back up that tree. This time he got about two-thirds of the way up the tree. But, what with that bottle bumping into the tree and bouncing off his belly, he lost his grip and slid back down to the ground. The third time, with great concentration and effort, the man and the bouncing bottle of common sense had almost completed their climb to the top when he stopped to catch his breath. That was when he heard a sound at the base of the tree and looked down to see a young man, maybe ten years old, looking up at him from the ground.

"Hey, mister," the boy called out, "it would be a lot easier for you to climb that tree if you would sling the bottle around your shoulder and carry it on your back."

Well, our friend with the get-rich-quick plan was so astounded with that boy's simple piece of common sense—a piece that he had over-looked in his search—that he lost his grip on the tree and fell to the ground. When he hit the ground with a thud, the bottle broke and com-mon sense burst out and floated all over the world. Most folks saw it floating around and they grabbed up pieces and stuffed it in their ears. As you probably can tell, some folks got more than others, but nobody was able to get it all for them-selves.

The truth is, some of it is still floating around, and I've noticed that you are pretty good at spotting it and stuffing it in your ears. That's one of the secrets. If you're going to make it, you have to keep getting smarter all the time.

SECRET NUMBER TWO:
FINANCIAL RESOURCES

Carlos came down the sidewalk, dribbling a basketball from hand to hand. Pete watched as Carlos unsuccessfully tried to slide the ball between his legs as he walked. His failure did not seem to darken his mood. He stopped in front of the steps where Pete sat in his usual spot and attempted to dribble behind his back. On the fourth try, he managed to keep control. He grabbed the ball with both hands and bounced it to his friend. Pete rolled the ball over in his hands and asked Carlos why it was that the ball had suddenly reappeared from Carlos' house.

"Would this have anything to do with free-agency in the NBA?" he asked with a grin.

"Are you kidding me? Did you see what The Dream and Shaq signed for?"

"You can't learn 'tall,'" Pete noted, remembering how Carlos had complained to him last week about being the smallest kid in his class.

"I know I'll never be seven feet. But Michael Jordan is going to get thirty million dollars for just one year. He must be richer than Michael Jackson!"

"There are some folks saying that Jordan is richer than God, and He owns the whole place."

Pete dribbled the ball three quick times on the step in front of him, then looked up at Carlos. "Some day, long after Jordan's basketball career is over, Michael is going to end up looking just like ol' Pete, except he'll probably still have both his eyes. There will be kids dribbling basketballs down the sidewalk who have never heard of Michael Jordan. When that day comes, it won't make any difference how much he made, it will only make a difference what he did with his skills and his money."

A Dozen Kernels of Corn

Back when I was a little boy, growing up in the country, my daddy told me a story about a man who lived north of town. This man not only had a big herd of cattle, but he also had four boys to help him run his farm. When the second world war broke out, the man decided he was needed by his country. Before he left for the war, he sat his sons down before him at the kitchen table. To each son he handed a small cloth bag. The boys untied the strings and emptied the contents of the bags onto the table. Twelve corn seeds fell out in front of each son.

"While I am gone," their father said, "I want you to take care of these special kernels of corn for me. When I return, I will ask you what has become of my gift."

One son took the twelve kernels of corn, and, realizing they must be very valuable, put them back in the cloth bag and placed the bag in a small wooden box. He then stuck the box underneath a loose plank in his bedroom floor. From time to time, he would pry that plank up and check on the corn because he wanted to make sure that nothing happened to it. When his father came home, he would be able to show his father that he had been able to safely protect his special gift.

Another son took an egg carton and painted the inside black. Then he took each kernel of corn and dropped it into the separate compartments of the carton. On Saturday morning he took the carton into town and secretly began to show the kernels of corn to people at the market. As he cracked open the lid of the egg carton, he told people about the power of the magic kernels that lay within. By the end of the day, the young man had managed to build quite a mystique around the "magic corn." Finally, he struck a deal with a city farmer, selling those twelve corn seeds for six hundred dollars. He took half the money and put it into the bank for his father. The other half he took for himself.

A third son took his small bag of seeds and left the farm behind. Eventually, he joined the navy and went off to the war. When the boy's ship was torpedoed, he was washed up onto a deserted island. On the verge of starvation, he ate those twelve kernels of corn in order to survive. Not long afterward, he was rescued and returned home.

The last son took those twelve kernels of corn and planted them in the garden behind the house. The plants grew tall and strong, and the son studied their growth, saving seeds to plant again. In time, he had carefully crossed those corn plants until he had a seed that produced a tall sturdy stalk on which grew large ears with many rows of kernels. His corn plants thrived in the dry August heat and also grew tall and strong in the rainiest of summers. Before long, the acres of corn that the boy planted not only fed the family's beef cattle, but also brought in large sums of money when sold to farmers throughout the South.

When the war ended, the boys celebrated their father's return to the farm. At the end of a welcome-home party, after neighbors and friends had all left, the father sat his boys down at the kitchen table and asked each one what had become of his gift to them.

The first son ran upstairs to his bedroom and returned with the wooden box. He opened the box and proudly handed the bag, with a dozen kernels of corn nestled inside, to his father.

The second son took out his wallet and counted out three crisp one hundred dollar bills. He then entertained his brothers and his father with the retelling of his tale of the "magic corn" seeds in the specially painted egg carton. He gave the money to his father but left out the part of the story where he decided to keep half the money for himself.

The third son told his father of his misfortune in the navy. He spoke of the torpedoed ship, the deserted island, and his near death from starvation. "It is because of your gift that I am here today to tell my story."

The fourth son smiled at his brothers and looked apologetically to his father. "I have neither corn nor money to return to you. I don't even have a good story to tell. But I did not let your gift go to waste."

The father looked out over his son's shoulder through the window at the fields of tall, sturdy green corn growing before him. "I see that you did not waste my gift," the father replied.

Then, looking at all his boys, he added,

"It's good to be home."

Each boy went on to live his own life, but it was the fourth son who inherited his father's farm.

Pete stood up and held Carlos' basketball in front of him. Then quickly he spun the ball up and balanced it on the tip of his index finger. He gave Carlos a big smile, popped the ball up into the air, and then flipped it behind his back to the wide-eyed boy on the sidewalk in front of him. "Remember, even Michael Jordan is going to grow old. We'll have to keep an eye on him—and see what he does with his money."

Pete turned, climbed the steps, and went into his house to get some lunch. Carlos stood on the sidewalk for the longest time, trying to spin the ball on the tip of his index finger.

SECRET NUMBER THREE:
EMOTIONAL RESOURCES

Pete heard the basketball dribbling as he opened the door and came out onto the step. He looked up the street toward the stop sign and smiled at the intense look of concentration that seemed to have enveloped his young friend this morning. Although Carlos did not appear to be a natural athlete, Pete believed that yesterday's practice may have improved his dribbling ever so slightly.

As Carlos approached, he heard Pete give a long admiring whistle. "You must have watched that ball game last night," said Pete.

Carlos looked up to answer and dribbled the ball off his foot. After he chased it down, Carlos sat down on the step to talk to Pete about his "hoops" plans. "Man, if I had a pair of those Air Jordans, I'd be twice as good as I am now. I would run faster, jump higher, and look better than the other kids in my class. And if I carried a bottle of that sports drink,

I'd be better than those kids all day long!"

"I think you need to find something else besides the shoes on your feet or the sports drink that you gulp," said Pete quietly, "if you're ever going to be a star basketball player."

One Whisker from the Wild Dog

A few years back, there was a woman in this neighborhood who fell in love with a man whose wife had died. Even though this man missed his wife, he knew he needed to find a mother for his son, so he turned to this woman. The woman moved in with the man and began to take care of the house and the boy. Now the man and his new wife could have been very happy, for they got along very well. But no matter what the woman did, she could not make the boy love her.

Each morning she would greet him with a hug, only to have the boy twist away and run out of the room. She would fix him his favorite food, but he would push the plate away and refuse to eat. She would talk to him about his day, and he would sit in stony silence. She would buy him things at the store, but he would ignore them, or break them, or throw them away. Finally, seeing how he drove a wedge between her and his father, the woman went to the tarot lady to ask for help.

In that little room behind the beauty shop, the tarot lady listened to the woman's trouble, read her cards, and then revealed the only way she could see to help her. "I can fix you a magic potion, but you will have to gather all the ingredients if it is going to work. Most of the ingredients you can get from your house or buy at the store, but the most important ingredient is one whisker from the nose of the wild dog."

Back then, everybody knew about the wild dog. The man at the junkyard had gotten this big old dog to guard his place. That dog was twice as big as the dog he has down there now, and three times as mean. The junkman had made that dog mean by teasing it, and beating it, and worse. One day that dog broke free from his chain and ran away. Even the animal shelter man was afraid to try to catch him. People would hear the dog roaming the streets at night, going through the garbage cans. A few people claimed they shot him. But they must not have been very good shots because that dog kept living by the bay in an old boat that had washed up during the last big storm.

Anyway, the tarot lady said she had to have a whisker from the wild dog if she was going to mix up a special potion to help the woman with  her stepson. That woman must have loved that boy and his daddy an awful lot, because she set out the next day to gather the ingredients for the potion. By the end of the day, she had all the fixings except the whisker from the wild dog.

Late that afternoon she walked out toward the bay. When she got about a quarter-mile from the wrecked boat, that huge dog stood up and stared at her from a distance. The woman took a piece of fresh meat out of a bag and laid it down on the ground. Then she backed up about a hundred yards and sat down to watch as the dog came out to snatch that meat and carry it back to his home.

The next afternoon the woman came back with her bag. This time she got to within an eighth of a mile before she put down the meat. Again she backed up, but only about fifty yards, and waited for the dog to come and grab that meat.

The next day she returned again, just like she did each and every day for weeks. Each day she moved a little closer before she put down the meat for the dog. Each day she stood closer as she watched that big dog come and snatch the meat up and carry it back to his home.

Finally, the woman was so close she knew that the next day she might get the final ingredient for her potion. Late the next afternoon, she found herself walking straight up to the dog's house above the bay. Slowly and surely, she walked to where the dog lay looking up at her. She bent down and took the meat from her bag, laying it carefully down in front of the dog's nose. As the dog raised his head and took the meat in his mouth, the woman reached out and plucked a single whisker from the dog's muzzle. She quietly thanked the beast, then turned and walked to town.

The woman went straight to the tarot shop and began to place the ingredients for the potion in front of the shopkeeper. Finally, she pulled the single whisker from her purse and laid it on the table. "There it is, the last of the ingredients!" she said proudly.

But the tarot lady answered even more proudly, "You have all the ingredients, but you no longer need the potion. If you approach your stepson the same way you approached the wild dog, the boy will grow to trust and love you."

Carlos thought about Pete's story for a while, rolling the basketball around in his hands. "Do you think that woman was hot when she found out she wouldn't get the potion?"

"No, I think she probably began to realize it's not always what you pour in from the outside that helps you make it, but what you discover on the inside."

"I think I would've been hot," Carlos replied. "All that work, and then not getting what the lady promised."

"Let me tell you about one time I didn't get what was promised to me."

The Single Flame (Part 1)

One winter, not long after I came to this neighborhood to live at my Uncle Frank's, we had one of those blue northers blow through town. The old men were sitting around a heater down at the barbershop complaining about how cold it was. It *was* pretty cold, but it wasn't cold enough to have to hear all the complaining. After all, I had spent a winter in Chicago once, after catching a ride north one fall to get a job with my Uncle Jamie in a steel mill on Lake Michigan. I never got on at the steel mills, and I had to take a job at a pool hall through the winter to get enough money to come home. I realized that one winter on Lake Michigan is worth a dozen down here.

Anyway, the old boys were all whining about how cold it was, and I said, "This is more like shirt-sleeve weather." They got all excited, commenting on how ignorant I was, and how I didn't know enough to come in out of the cold. You know how they talk.

I had gone down to the barbershop with a neighborhood buddy who was a year or two older than I and quite a bit hipper.

He punched me in the arm and said, "Tell

60

these old whiners about that icy winter up north."

So I got all puffed up and told them about how cold it had been that winter in Chicago and made the mistake of comparing the current conditions to a summer evening. That really got them going. They made a few more derogatory statements about my mental health. Within moments, I proved them to be right on target.

"If you think this is shirt-sleeve weather," one of them said, exasperated with my insistence that it wasn't cold out, "I'll bet you a free dinner that you can't spend the night outside tonight with no coat, and no means of heat."

"Sure he can," my running buddy replied. "This cold is nothing to him."

Like a fool, I took them up on the bet, and that evening when the sun went down, they all sat inside their places, including my good buddy who got me into the bet. I stood out on the street corner, my back to the north wind, shivering in my short-sleeve shirt. I would've given up and gone inside by ten o'clock, but I kept myself warm thinking about how broke and embarrassed I would be when I lost the bet and had to have all those old men over to my Uncle Frank's place for dinner.

By midnight, I was fixin' to freeze to death and no longer cared if I lost the bet. I stepped off the curb and started to cross the street toward home, when I heard a big whoosh! The refinery started burning off chemicals, and one of those

huge flares was lighting up the sky west of the neighborhood. I stepped back up onto the curb and looked at that flare burning brightly some two miles away. For the rest of the night I locked my eyes onto that single flame, taking its light and heat past my eyes and into my heart. Somehow, that fire burning way across town helped me make it through the cold night. I learned that night that, sometimes, it's not the heat you get from the outside that helps you make it in this world. It's the fire that burns from inside.

SECRET NUMBER FOUR:
ROLE MODELS

"So, when you won the bet, where did they take you for dinner?" Carlos asked.

"Well, sir," Pete replied, "that's another story altogether."

The Single Flame (Part 2)

The next morning, when my running buddy came out to congratulate me, we headed across the street to where the old men had gathered at the doughnut shop. The little bell on the inside of the door announced my arrival. The men all glanced over at me, standing there in my shirt sleeves with a smile on my face. I was planning on which restaurant they would have to take me to that night for losing the bet.

They didn't like losing the bet, but they were pretty impressed with my tolerance of the cold. One of them asked me if it had ever crossed my mind to give up and come inside. Candidly, I told them about how I had indeed given up and was heading in when the refinery flare shot up at midnight. They listened as I explained how I watched that single flame all through the rest of the night.

"Well, there you have it!" Red said. "What time do you want us to come for dinner tonight?"

"I was planning on you taking *me* to dinner," I shot back. "I won the bet."

"Oh, no, you didn't. The bet was that you could stay out all night with no coat and no means of heat. But you just told us that the flame down at the refinery is what kept you warm. So, you lose the bet. You can expect us for dinner tonight at seven."

I turned to my buddy to back me up, but he just shrugged his shoulders and said, "I guess they got you on that one."

If there had been any cold left in me from the long night, it was gone by the time I got to my Uncle Frank's house. I was hot. They were supposed to take me out to dinner, and now I had to tell my Uncle Frank all about how I lost the bet. I had to tell him I would be needing the kitchen that night and some money to buy food. Then we would have to put up with all those conniving old men for dinner.

"And all because you got too big for your britches and couldn't keep your big mouth shut!" my Uncle Frank said.

I threw myself down in a chair and sat there seething for a while. Finally, my Uncle Frank came over, sat down next to me, and gave me a conspiratorial wink.

"How about we try it this way?" he said, and he unfolded his plan.

That evening, around seven o'clock, the old men began to gather in the front room at my Uncle Frank's. Frank talked to the men while I busied myself running in and out of the kitchen door, excusing myself to check on dinner, returning to the conversation, jumping back up to go into the kitchen. Frank was telling them about how he and his brothers had put up with years of cold winters up in Illinois. However, the old men were having trouble listening to Frank's tales because they were distracted by the growling of their stomachs.

One of the old men finally asked, "Is that dinner about ready?"

"It's cooking," I promised. I jumped up and

ran into the kitchen to check on it.

Finally, after two or three more of Frank's stories, old Red commented, "I don't smell anything cooking. Why don't we all go into the kitchen to check and see how dinner is coming?"

When he stood up, all those old men stood up with him, and together they walked over and swung open the kitchen door.

There at eye level in the middle of the kitchen was a pot of beans hanging from a rope tied to the kitchen light. On the floor, about five feet below, a candle was burning.

Before anyone else could speak, I explained, "I'm trying to heat up our dinner, but it's going sort of slow."

Red was the first to reply. "That's the dumbest thing I ever saw. There is no way that candle is going to be able to cook those beans!"

My Uncle Frank stepped forward and looked all those old men in the eye. "Why, surely, gentlemen," he said, "if the flame of that refinery flare can warm Pete all night from two miles away, the flame of this candle ought to be able to warm our dinner from a mere distance of five feet!"

There was a moment of silence, then Red

turned to me: "Why don't you and your uncle get your coats? We'll take you up to Main Street and buy you a barbecue dinner."

"Your Uncle Frank sure bailed you out of that one," Carlos said, shaking his head and smiling.

"The real help came later that evening when we were coming home," replied Pete.

Getting Out of a Load of Trouble

Uncle Frank looked up into the night sky, pulled his coat tight around his neck, and cleared his throat. I knew he was about to say something serious. He always cleared his throat like that before he gave advice.

"When I was a boy," he said, "I was walking down Lakeway Drive with my daddy late in the afternoon on a cold, cold day. We looked up at a flock of geese flying overhead. There was a big V in the sky, but the whole flock was fighting against the wind. We could see one bird at the end of the V fall back and lose altitude. Within moments, we watched that bird take a dive and land stiffly in the gutter of the street. It was obvious the poor thing was nearly frozen to death, and we knew that it would soon die. Before we could decide what to do for that pitiful creature, a horse-drawn wagon came up the street, and the driver pulled his rig up to the curb. The goose was barely spared being crushed beneath the huge hoofs of that draft horse.

"As the wagon came to a stop, the horse relieved himself, dumping a load on the head of that frozen bird. Moments later, the wagon headed on down the street. My father and I stared as that steaming mound in the street began to quiver, and happy sounds began to emanate from its interior. Again, before we even could think what to do, a stray dog came out of an alley and, perking his ears at the sound, began to sniff  around the pile in the street. That bony mutt pawed twice at the edge of the pile, then knocked off the top, grabbed the goose by the neck, and carried him away.

"My father watched as the dog, with bird clamped in his jaw, disappeared up the alley. Then he looked down at me and said, 'Let that be a lesson to you, son. It's not always your enemies who dump on you, nor is it always your friends who get you out of a stinking mess. And until you can learn the difference between the two, it's best to keep your mouth shut.'"

"Uncle Frank was lucky enough to have his daddy to steer him through, and I was lucky to have my Uncle Frank," said Pete. "If you are fortunate, you will have people around you who can show you the ropes and make your way easier. If you are not fortunate, you just have to be smart. Find good people to learn from and stay clear of those who will steer you wrong."

SECRET NUMBER FIVE:
SUPPORT SYSTEMS

Carlos was mumbling under his breath when he plopped down on the step .

"What's up?" Pete asked.

"They all make me sick!"

"Who makes you sick?"

"All of them! The kids at school ... the teachers ... my mother. All of them!"

"They all make you sick? Be careful now, you may need some of those people."

"Man, I don't need any of those sorry folks. I don't need anybody!"

Pete waited for a while, giving Carlos some time to calm down. Then he said quietly, "That's one of the problems in this world. It's also one of the secrets to making it. Sometimes you just don't know who you can count on. There are some who will come through for you, and some who won't. A person needs to find out who will be there when the times are

tough. *When you know who those people are, you
need to take care of them. One day, you might need
them to take care of you."*

Spread Your Fingers When You Eat

Back when the steel mill closed down, there
were a lot of people who lost their jobs. One man
in the neighborhood was taking care of his first
wife and his new wife. When he lost his job, he
went back to the little town where he grew up
and went to work on a truck farm, picking and
packing fruits and vegetables to sell at the farmers' market in the city. Every time he brought a
load into market, he would stop in the neighborhood and leave food for his wives.

Each time he dropped off the food for his
wives, he would remind each one to "make sure
you spread your fingers when you eat." Now the
first wife did not understand very well what he
meant when he said that.

But the new wife was wiser than the first
and understood that when he brought her food,
she was not to eat alone, but always to share her
food with others who had less than she did. That

is what her husband meant when he said to spread her fingers when she ate.

Now the first wife, what she cooked, she ate. And she always ate alone. After she had finished eating she went outside, held her hands out in front of her, and stretched her fingers wide apart. "My ex-  husband told me to spread my fingers when I eat," she said to herself.

He brought her strawberries and raspberries and peaches and apples. He brought her corn and okra and collard greens and black-eyed peas. Sometimes he even brought her bacon and salt ham. But she always ate it alone.

The new wife got the same fruits and vegetables and, sometimes, the meats. But whenever he brought her the food, she would look around her and make sure that she shared her food with a brother or uncle or neighbor or the preacher's family or the old woman who lived next door.

About two years after the steel mill closed,

people were just beginning to get on their feet again when word came that the man had been killed in an accident on the farm. Of course, lots of folks in the neighborhood were sad to hear about that. But none were as sad as the man's two wives. The first wife—the one who spread her fingers in the air after she ate—sat at home alone and didn't hear from anybody. But many people visited and brought things to the wife who freely shared her food. One brought vegetables, another a chicken, another fish, and still another sugar and coffee. The gifts continued to be given as she mourned the death of her husband.

One day the first wife came to visit the second and, seeing all those who came to help, she said, "Sister, ever since our man died, I have been hungry; no one brought me anything. But look how many people have brought you things to help you survive."

The second wife asked the first, "When my husband brought you things to eat, what did you do with them?"

"I ate them," she answered.

"When my husband said to you, 'Spread your fingers when you eat,' what did you do?"

"Each meal, when I was finished eating, I stretched my fingers in the air."

The second wife laughed. "Then the air must bring you your food, because that is where you spread your fingers. As for me, the same people I gave food to now bring me gifts in return."

Before the first wife left, the second wife offered her half of her dinner.

Pete looked at Carlos for a long time after he finished his story. "When your auntie needs help, does your mama ever turn her away?"

"No, sir!" Carlos answered, with a touch of pride in his voice.

"When Mrs. Martin's Joshua went to jail, did your mama help her out?"

"Yes, sir," Carlos said, suddenly lapsing into thought.

"And when you and your mama are in trouble, like last year when your mama got sick and couldn't work, did people come busting in to help you out?"

"Yep, they sure did."

"Well, Carlos, you'd better be careful counting out people you don't need. After all, it's having people you can count on that's one of the secrets to making it."

"One thing for sure," Carlos said, "I can always count on you for a story."

"If I ever lose my voice, like I lost my eye," Pete said with a grin, "I'll have to count on you to tell the stories."

SECRET NUMBER SIX:
SPIRITUAL RESOURCES

Carlos was still doubting that he had the tools to make it. "You say I'm going to be fine," he said to Pete, "but I'm not sure I believe it."

"Well, that is a problem. You have just hit on one of the secrets. If you're going to make it, you have to believe."

Carlos looked up into Pete's good eye. "What

do I have to believe in?"

"I won't tell you that," Pete replied. "I'll only tell you that you have to believe."

The Bleacher Bum

You remember last month when I went to see the Astros play? The Braves were in town. I took the community center bus, and we sat over on the first-base side beyond the dugout. Right in front of us, in about the third row from the bottom, there was a bunch a kids about your age. It looked to me like they were there for a birthday party. They were all lined up in one row. Several of them had on Astros caps, and most of them were more interested in the hot dogs than the ball game. One lady—I figured she was the birthday boy's mom—sat one row back trying to keep up with all those kids and make sure they had a good time.

It wasn't a great game. The Astros were losing by four or five runs and, by the seventh inning, some of the fans were starting to leave. Right after the seventh-inning stretch, one of the boys who was sitting pretty far down the row stood up and crawled over the other boys to get to the aisle. Then he told the birthday boy's mom that he had to go to the bathroom. He had no sooner headed up the steps than a great big lumbering man came down the same steps with an old baseball glove on his hand. He stopped at the end of that third row and proceeded to climb over all those kids until he got to the open seat that the child left when he went up to the bathroom.

All of us sitting behind leaned forward to see what would happen next. This was the most interesting thing we had seen since the second inning when three Braves in a row struck out. It was clear that the woman was uncomfortable with that stranger taking a seat in the middle of her party. But there he sat, a big man-child, smiling and popping his glove with the fist of his other hand. She finally moved over a few seats to her right, bent forward, and tapped the man on his shoulder. We could tell she was trying to explain to the man that the seat was taken, that the boy the seat belonged to had gone to the bathroom. She even turned and pointed back toward the stairs and the exit. The man seemed to listen to the whole explanation, smiling and nodding all the while. But when the lady finished her little speech, the man turned around with that big joyful grin on his face and continued thumping his glove with his fist.

The mom turned toward us with a hopeless look on her face. I think she was about to get an usher or someone from security when the Braves' clean-up hitter smacked a screaming line drive directly toward our section. Before we could even react, that big fellow in the third row reached

out and caught the ball right before it would have smashed into the face of the boy sitting next to him. Everyone in our section sat in stunned silence, but the rest of the crowd gave the man a big cheer. He never stopped smiling. He sat there a moment, popping that baseball into his old mitt, then turned and handed the ball to the birthday boy. Without saying a word, he stood up and climbed over the rest of the folks in the row, lumbered up the steps two at a time, and disappeared into the stadium.

Within a minute, the boy who had gone to the bathroom returned to the third row, climbed over his friends, and sat back down in his empty seat. For the rest of the ball game, that lady kept turning around to us and saying, "Did you see that? That man saved that boy's life. He must have been sent by God. Do you think that man was an angel?"

By the end of the game she was telling anyone who would listen about the stranger who caught the line drive. "I believe that man was an angel!" she kept repeating.

"Do you believe he was an angel?" Carlos asked Pete when he was sure the story was over.

"Doesn't make any difference whether I believe it or not. That lady believed it. She took that little boy back to his family safe and sound. You have to decide for yourself what you believe. But you have to believe in something if you're planning on making it in this world."

SECRET NUMBER SEVEN:
PHYSICAL RESOURCES

Seeing Carlos walk down the street at nine in the morning on a school day was a little disturbing to Pete. As Carlos headed across the street toward him, Pete noticed that his young friend had a plastic milk bottle in one hand and a stick with some rope on it in the other.

"I have two questions for you," Pete said with a furrowed brow. "What are you doing out of school? And what in the world is that stuff you have in your hands?"

Carlos was quick to answer the first question, knowing how many times Pete had talked to him about the importance of his schoolwork. "Today is one of those teacher-training days. The teachers have to go to work, but we get the day off. Mama took the bus to the hospital to see Grandma, and I'm on my own."

"Trying to stay out of trouble?"

"Trying to," Carlos answered.

"That stuff in your hands ... is that supposed to help?"

Carlos dropped the milk bottle at his feet with a clunk. Pete noticed that it was filled with rocks and sand. As Carlos bent over and tied the rope to the bottle handle, he began to answer Pete's second question.

"I thought today would be a good day to start weight-training," Carlos began. Pete reached to scratch his nose, wanting to hide his smile from this scrawny little friend who stood in front of him. Carlos continued in earnest.

"I figure I've got ten to fifteen pounds in that bottle. I can unroll this rope to different lengths and do all kinds of weight-lifting. If I work out long enough, I can have one of those bodies that looks 'chiseled.' Just because I'm little doesn't mean I have to be puny."

"Your body is a temple. That's what the Bible says. It never hurts to work out. That's one of life's secrets. You need to find out what you're good at and work hard to stay good at it. You never know when your skill will come in handy."

By now Carlos was holding that piece of broomstick in front of him, with the rope tied to the milk bottle at his feet. He began to curl the stick up to his chin as Pete sat down on the step and started a story.

"Once upon a time there was a boy named Carlos ..."

"Are you sure his name was Carlos?" asked Carlos with a quick sideways glance, easing the bottle back down to the sidewalk.

"That was his name," answered Pete.

Carlos and the Flying Boat

Once upon a time there was a boy named Carlos. One day Carlos had the day off from school. His mother went to the hospital to visit Carlos' grandma. Before she left home, she told Carlos to keep an eye on the house and not to go wandering off with his friends.

"Okay, Mama," Carlos said.

After Carlos' mother left, Carlos' friends Terry and Seth came by the house to watch TV. They sat up and paid close attention when a "beep, beep, beep" alerted them to a special report on the TV. A newsman came on to announce that the governor's daughter had been kidnapped by a strange conjure-man. The governor had offered a hundred thousand dollars to anyone who could return his daughter safely.

"Wow, that's a lot of money. I believe I'm going to go look for that girl," Terry said. "You guys want to go with me?"

"My mama said I had to keep an eye on the house," Carlos commented, after seriously considering the invitation. Seth decided it might be wise to stay with Carlos. So they packed Terry a lunch with some tuna fish, an apple, some candy, and a can of Big K Cola. Then Terry started off to find the governor's daughter.

He hadn't gone too far when he decided to sit down and eat his lunch. An old woman with a cane in one hand and a shopping bag in the other tottered along the sidewalk and sat down next to him. "Can you share some of your meal, sonny boy?"

"Are you kidding?" said Terry with a laugh. "You'll have to find your food somewhere else. I have to eat all this so I'll be strong enough to take on the powerful conjure-man who stole the governor's daughter."

"That must be the conjure-man who lives on the other side of the railroad tracks," said the old woman with a knowing look.

Terry was in such a hurry to save the governor's daughter he didn't even finish his lunch. He threw half his tuna fish into the trash can and headed toward the railroad tracks. When he got to the conjure-man's house, he knocked on the front door. When nobody answered, Terry tiptoed around to the backyard. Suddenly, out popped the conjure-man.

"What are you doing snooping around my yard?"

Terry said, "I came to break the conjure spell and save the governor's daughter."

"If you want to save the governor's daughter, you have to pass four tests. This is the first one."

The conjure-man looped a rope around his guard dog's neck, then took off the dog's spiked collar and laid it on the ground. The conjure-man climbed up on a bucket and leapt onto the spiked collar headfirst. He popped up smiling, just like he had landed on a pillow.

"Your turn," the conjure-man said to Terry.

Terry climbed up on the bucket, closed his eyes, dove through the air, and landed on the spikes. "OOWWW! I broke my head!" he wailed. Terry ran all the way back to Carlos' house, holding his hand over a bleeding head wound. Carlos and Seth, who had just seen a wound of this sort on "Emergency 911," bandaged up Terry's head and put him on the couch.

"Dang," Seth grumbled. "We can't let that conjure-man do this to our friend. I'm going to go save that governor's daughter and fix him good. How about packing me a lunch before I go?"

Carlos fixed Seth a lunch with tuna fish, an apple, some candy, and a can of Big K Ginger Ale. Then Seth started off to find the governor's daughter.

He hadn't gone very far when he decided to sit down and eat his lunch. He was about to start eating when an old woman with a cane in one hand and a shopping bag in the other tottered along the sidewalk and sat down next to him. "Can you share some of your meal, sonny boy?"

"Are you kidding?" Seth replied. "You'll have to find your food somewhere else. I have to eat all this myself so I'll be strong enough to take on the powerful conjure-man who stole the governor's daughter."

"That must be the conjure-man who lives on the other side of the railroad tracks," the old woman commented.

Seth was in such a hurry to save the governor's daughter he didn't even finish his lunch. He threw half his tuna fish into the trash can and headed toward the railroad tracks. When he got to the conjure-man's house, he knocked on the front door. When nobody answered, Seth tiptoed around to the backyard. Suddenly, out popped the conjure-man.

"What are you doing snooping around my yard?"

Seth said, "I came to break the conjure spell and save the governor's daughter."

"If you want to save the governor's daughter, you have to pass four tests. This is the first one."

The conjure-man once again looped a rope around his guard dog's neck, then took off the dog's spiked collar and laid it on the ground. The conjure-man climbed up on a bucket and leapt onto the spiked collar headfirst. He popped up smiling, just like he had landed on a bag of down feathers.

"Your turn," the conjure-man said to Seth.

Seth climbed up on the bucket, closed his eyes, dove through the air, and landed on the spikes. "OOWWW! I broke my head!" he screamed. Seth ran all the way back to Carlos' house, holding his hand over his bleeding head wound. Carlos had just taken Terry home and heard him tell his mom a story about how he had fallen off a bike and hit his head. Now he put a bandage on Seth's gash and laid him on the couch.

"You have to go save the governor's daughter and get even with that conjure-man for us," Seth mumbled to Carlos.

"Okay," Carlos answered. "Promise to keep an eye on the house for me?" Seth said he would.

Carlos tried to fix himself a lunch before he left, but he was all out of tuna fish, apples, candy, and Big K cold drinks. So he took some old bread and a bottle of tap water and started off to find the governor's daughter.

He hadn't gone very far when he decided to stop and eat his sorry old lunch. Just then an old woman with a cane in one hand and a shopping bag in the other tottered along the sidewalk and sat down next to him. "Can you share some of your meal, sonny boy?"

"It's not much of a meal," Carlos answered, "but you're welcome to join me."

The old woman sat down, and Carlos gave her some bread and half of his water. When they were finished eating, the old woman said, "You are a fine young man, Carlos, and I bet your mama is proud of you." She fumbled through her shopping bag and pulled out an old piece of tire tread. "I know this looks like an old chunk of tire that I picked up off the street, but it's a magic piece of tire tread. You just hold it in front of you, toss it up in the air, and say, 'Fly, boat, fly,' and that tire tread will take you wherever you want to go. So now that we're finished eating, why don't you sail off and save the governor's daughter? That conjure-man lives right over there on the other side of the railroad tracks."

Carlos thanked the old woman and headed down the street toward the railroad tracks to find the conjure-man's house and save the governor's daughter. He threw his lunch bag into the trash and was surprised when two big alley cats came leaping out of the garbage can. Before he got to the conjure-man's house, he decided to try out his magic tire tread. He held it out in front of him, closed his eyes, tossed it up in the air, and said, "Fly, boat, fly." When he opened his eyes, he saw that little piece of tire get bigger and bigger until there, floating in the air in front of him,

was a forty-five-foot cabin cruiser, with a horn and a radar and nautical flags flapping in the breeze. The anchor line came down and was hooked onto a stop sign.

Carlos jumped into his magic boat, pulled in the anchor chain, and said, "Fly, boat, fly," and that boat went up into the blue sky. Pretty soon Carlos could see the whole city below him—his mama's house on one side, the conjure-man's house on the other and, way off in the distance, he thought he could see the governor's mansion. As he was gazing off to the north, he suddenly heard a strange sound below him.

He looked over the side of the boat and, down below, saw a boy running along a road as fast as he could, bumping his head into telephone poles so that all the wires shook—up and down the line.

Carlos yelled down, "Yo, Bro! What's up?"

"Looks like you're up!"

"Nope. It's Texas! Wanna see from up here?"

"Sure. Why not?"

When the boy came on the boat, Carlos stood up straight, extended his right hand, and said, "My name's Carlos; welcome to my flying boat."

The boy shook Carlos' hand and replied, "My name's Carlton. My friends call me 'Concrete Cranium.' I'm pleased to meet you."

Carlos smiled, gunned the motor, and off they went.

After a while, Carlos heard another sound. They looked over the side of the boat and, down below, saw a boy running across a golf course. Every time he got to a water hole, he would bend down and drink it dry with one gulp. Then he would pick up all the golf balls left in the mud, throw them in a bag, and go to the next hole.

Carlos yelled down, "Yo, Bro! What's up?"

"Looks like you're up!"

"Nope. It's Texas! Wanna see from up here?"

"Sure. Why not?"

When the boy came on the boat, Carlos stood up straight, extended his right hand, and said, "My name's Carlos; welcome to my flying boat."

The boy shook Carlos' hand and replied, "My name's Slurpitup, the used-golf-ball salesman. I'm pleased to meet you."

Carlos smiled, gunned the motor, and off they went.

Suddenly, they heard another sound. They looked over the side of the boat and saw another boy running across the golf course. He was racing from mudhole to mudhole, picking up big old catfish with two hands and swallowing them like they were no more than a candy mint.

Carlos yelled down, "Yo, Bro! What's up?"

"Looks like you're up!"

"Nope. It's Texas! Wanna see from up here?"

"Sure. Why not?"

When the boy came on the boat, Carlos stood up straight, extended his right hand, and said, "My name's Carlos; welcome to my flying boat."

The boy shook Carlos' hand and replied, "My name's Gary Gobble. I'm pleased to meet you." They were just about to set off when they saw three girls standing on top of a hill. The first girl was listening with her hand cupped over her ear.

Carlos shouted down, "Hey, what do you hear?"

"I just heard a Ford Taurus run over an armadillo on a stretch of highway five hundred miles away."

"Wow! What's your name?"

"Heargood. What's yours?"

"My name's Carlos. Want to come on my boat?"

"Sure. Why not?"

Heargood got on the boat.

The second girl was gazing into the distance, her hands shading her eyes. Carlos said to her, "What do you see?"

"I see a buzzard swooping down to eat a dead armadillo squished on a highway five hundred miles away."

"What's your name?"

"Seegood. What's yours?"

"My name's Carlos. Want to come on my boat?"

"Sure. Why not?"

So Seegood got on the boat.

The third girl was sniffing the air. Carlos said to her, "What do you smell?"

"I smell the breath of a buzzard choking on a piece of armadillo five hundred miles away."

"What's your name?"

"Smellgood. What's yours?"

"My name's Carlos. Want to come on my boat?"

"Sure. Why not?"

Smellgood got on the boat, too.

They were just about to sail away when— bang!— they heard a shot. They all ducked down, then Carlos peeked over the side of the boat and saw a man with a rifle in his hand, smoke coming out of the barrel.

Carlos said, "Hey mister, what did you shoot?"

"I just put a buzzard out of its misery five hundred miles away."

"What's your name?"

"Sureshot. What's yours?"

"My name's Carlos. Want to come on my boat?"

"Sure. Why not?"

Sureshot got on the boat with Carlos and the others. Carlos smiled, gunned the motor, and off they went. After a while, they heard another sound. They looked over the side of the boat and, down below, they saw a girl running around the track at the high school so fast you could barely see her. She was just a blur. Carlos yelled down to her, "Yo, Sister! What's up?"

"Looks like Europe!"

"Nope. It's Texas! Wanna see from up here?"

"Sure. Why not?"

When the girl came on the boat, Carlos

stood up straight, extended his right hand, and said, "My name's Carlos; welcome to my flying boat."

The girl shook Carlos' hand and replied, "My name's Veronica, but my friends call me Speed Demon."

Carlos said, "Enough of this messing around. My mama is going to be home from the hospital soon. I've got to go save the governor's daughter." He smiled, gunned the motor, and off they went.

They flew across the railroad tracks, and he sailed the boat down and down and down until they landed in the conjure-man's backyard. When Carlos got out of the boat, out popped the conjure-man.

"What are you doing docking that boat to snoop around my yard?"

Carlos said, "I came to break the conjure spell and save the governor's daughter."

"If you want to save the governor's daughter, you have to pass four tests. This is the first one."

The conjure-man looped that rope around his guard dog's neck, then took off the dog's

spiked collar and laid it on the ground. The conjure-man climbed up on a bucket and leapt onto
the spiked collar headfirst. He popped up smiling, just like he had landed on Carlos' mama's
fluffy house slippers.

"Your turn," the conjure-man said.

"Well," said Carlos, "I believe my friend
Carlton with the concrete cranium will stand in
for me on this one."

Carlton got out of the boat, stood on the
bucket, dove through the air doing a triple somersault with a twist in the pike position and landed
headfirst on the spike collar, breaking it into a
thousand pieces.

"So you passed the first test, but you still
have three to go," the conjure-man said angrily.
"Now, do you have anybody who likes to drink?"

"Well," Carlos said, "my friend Slurpitup
takes an occasional sip of water."

Slurpitup got out of the boat.

"Slurpitup," the conjure-man said, "here
are two creeks. That one will be yours, and this
one is mine. We'll race to see who can drink his
creek dry first." The conjure-man began to drink,
but before he was half finished, Slurpitup had

drunk his whole creek dry and, not finding any golf balls, had begun to drink from the conjure-man's creek, hoping it was closer to the golf course.

"So you've passed two of the four tests," the conjure-man said. "There are still two more tests to go."

"Man, this is worse than school," Carlos moaned. "What's the next test?"

"You got anybody who likes to eat?"

"My friend Gary Gobble has been known to enjoy food," Carlos said.

Gary got out of the boat. The conjure-man motioned toward two refrigerator trucks across the street in the parking lot of a meat-packing plant. "We're going to see who can eat all the meat in his truck first." The trucks were opened, and they dug in. When Gary Gobble was finished with all the meat in his truck, the conjure-man was only halfway through with his.

"You got anything for dessert?" Gary asked.

"All right. So you've passed three of the four tests. Lots of people have done that. But I doubt that you have anybody who can beat me in this next test. Do you have anybody who likes to run?"

"My friend Veronica jogs a little bit," Carlos said.

"We're going to see who can run the fastest from here to the Pacific Ocean and back again—twelve hundred miles over and twelve hundred miles back."

The conjure-man held out two paper cups. He handed one cup to Veronica. "Fill your paper cup with saltwater to prove that you have been to the Pacific Ocean. Ready, set, go!"

The conjure-man took off like a shot, but Veronica flew by that old conjure-man like he was tied to a post. She ran all the way to the Pacific Ocean, filled her cup with saltwater, and headed back home. She was about halfway over the Rocky Mountains on the way back when she met the conjure-man running toward the Pacific.

The conjure-man knew he was going to have to cheat in order to win, so he reached into his pocket, pulled out a bottle of nitric oxide (his brother was a dentist), and waited at the side of the path. When Veronica ran by he said, "Stop! Stop! Do you want a little oxygen to help you make it through the mountains?"

"Gee, how thoughtful," she said.

The conjure-man slipped that mask over her nose and mouth and turned on the gas. She was sound asleep by the count of ten. With a wicked laugh, the conjure-man sprinted off to the Pacific Ocean to fill his cup with salt water.

Meanwhile, Carlos and his friends became worried. Carlos said to Smellgood, "Something stinks here. Anything in the wind?"

"I smell nitric oxide nine hundred miles away."

"Heargood, what's on the wind?"

Heargood cupped a hand to her ear. "Uh-oh! I believe Veronica might be sleeping on the job. I hear snoring nine hundred miles away."

"Seegood, what do you spy?"

"Bad news, Carlos. Veronica is sound asleep on the ground with a mask over her face. I don't believe she's ever going to wake up."

"Don't be so sure," said Sureshot. He raised his rifle to his shoulder and squeezed the trigger. KAPOW! The bullet traveled nine hundred miles and struck the nitric-oxide canister, knocking it off Veronica's face. As soon as she got a breath of that clear, cool, Rocky Mountain air, she woke up, looked around, and saw that her cup was empty. She headed back to the Pacific Ocean for a refill.

In the meantime, the conjure-man was running for the finish. As he neared town, Veronica appeared on the horizon. She was running as fast has she could. Soon they were running neck and neck! At the last second, Veronica lunged forward into the backyard and won the race.

She handed Carlos the cup of saltwater and said, "They don't call me Speed Demon for nothing."

The conjure-man looked at Carlos and his friends. "You won fair and square, and that really makes me mad. But a deal is a deal." He took them around to the back of the shed and unlocked the door. Out came the governor's daughter, looking a little bit confused by the appearance of Carlos and his strange friends.

They loaded her onto the magic boat and took her to the governor's mansion, where they were given the cash reward and honored with a barbecue dinner. Then Carlos and his friends spent the rest of the day cruising around in the magic boat. And, you know, Carlos got back home just in time for ...

Carlos looked up. The city bus was braking for the bus stop at the corner of the street. "I got to run, Pete. That's Mama's bus. She's already home from the hospital. I wonder how Grandma is doing."

As Carlos started down the street, Pete yelled after him, "Run fast, look sharp, listen well, and—hey—watch out for those telephone poles."

QUESTIONS: CHAPTER 3
Referring to Resources

Secret Number One: Mental Resources

Common Sense

1. What does it mean to "get smarter all the time"?

2. How does being able to read, write, count, add, and subtract make you leaner and meaner?

3. How do you know when someone is smarter? What is the difference between street-smart and book-smart?

4. Can you be a real man and be book-smart?

5. How does what is "inside your head" keep you from being cheated?

6. What can you do to be smarter?

Secret Number Two: Financial Resources

A Dozen Kernels of Corn

1. Which son used his money the best? How can money help you? How can money hurt you?

2. Is having money bad? Is it bad to be rich?

3. Some people believe money is to be shared and spent. Some people believe money is for having fun. Some believe it is for buying things. Some believe it is to use for the betterment of groups of people. What do you believe about money?

4. How would you make money? How would you save money?

5. People with more education usually make more money. How could you get more education?

6. When you get money, what do you do with it?

Secret Number Three: Emotional Resources

One Whisker from the Wild Dog

1. Emotional resources are those resources inside of people that help them when times are rough. When people have emotional resources, they make it through the tough times without drugs, without being violent, and without hurting themselves or others. The woman in "One Whisker from the Wild Dog" has patience. How do you know that?

2. Why does the woman keep going back to the wild dog? Has there been anything you have wanted that you have been willing to go to a great amount of effort to get?

3. What do you do when you're feeling discouraged? Lonely? Unloved?

4. Many people turn to alcohol and drugs as a way to deal with rough times. What happens when they do? Does this solve problems?

5. What can you say to yourself inside your head to make it through the rough times?

6. Persistence (to keep trying even after you fail) is a key predictor of people who are successful. Albert Einstein failed in elementary school. Abraham Lincoln was defeated in several elections before he became President. Thomas Edison tried more than a hundred different kinds of light bulbs before he found one that would work. What would you be willing to try again and again?

The Single Flame (Part 1)

1. What does this story mean?

2. What flame burns inside of you? What do you keep working for, no matter how dark and cold the night?

3. Write down something you would like to do or have in five years. Make a picture of that inside your head.

Secret Number Four: Role Models

The Single Flame (Part 2)

1. Why do people not want to give credit to someone who is emotionally strong?

2. Why does emotional strength sometimes require a person to take a position different from his or her friends?

3. Pete kept warm by keeping his eye on the flame. What do you have your eye on that will keep you going even when it's lonely and dark?

4. Many people go through times in their lives that are very difficult. What are the different things people do to get through bad times, without hurting themselves or others?

5. What picture do you keep in your head to help you when times are difficult? What do you say to yourself?

6. When friends are going through bad times, what advice do you give to them?

Getting Out of a Load of Trouble

1. How do you know when someone is a friend?

2. How do you know when someone is an enemy?

3. Stephen Covey states in one of his books that we have relationships with people because they have given us "emotional" money. When they give us more than they take from us, we have a relationship with them. When they take more than they give, we are broke or bankrupt and do not want to be friends with them anymore. Ways people give us "emotional" money include: (1) by seeking to understand first, (2) by giving kindness and being courteous, (3) by not talking about people when they aren't there,

(4) by being clear what we can and cannot do, (5) by apologizing, and (6) by keeping promises. We take away "emotional" money when we do the opposite of the things above. Think of a relationship you have right now. What is one thing you could do to give that relationship "emotional" money?

4. What do you do when a "friend" is really an enemy?

5. On the street you are respected if you are physically stronger than your enemy. Often that respect is established through a physical fight. What are other ways to show strength?

Secret Number Five: Support Systems

Spread Your Fingers When You Eat

1. A support system includes all those people you help or who help you. Who are the people in your support system?

2. Who are the people for whom you are a support system?

3. What kind of other people would you like in your support system? How would you go about getting them to be a part of your support system?

4. In the story the first wife doesn't work to create a support system. She lives only for herself. The second wife creates a support system. Why does the second wife offer the first wife half of her dinner at the end of the story? Would you do that?

Secret Number Six: Spiritual Resources

The Bleacher Bum

1. Do you believe in God—or a source of divine power or help?

2. What does it mean at the end of the story when Pete says, "Doesn't make any difference whether I believe it or not. That lady believed it. She took that little boy back to his family safe and sound. You have to decide for yourself what you believe. But you have to believe in something if you're planning on making it in this world"?

3. What do you believe is the purpose of your life?

Secret Number Seven: Physical Resources

Carlos and the Flying Boat

1. Physical resources are the means by which you stay alive and take care of yourself. Each of the characters in this story has a physical resource. What are these physical resources? What physical resources do you have?

2. Some people are physically strong. Some are healthy; they rarely get sick. Some can go hours without sleep. Some see well. Some hear well. Some are coordinated. Some have dexterity (they can make anything with their hands). Some have beautiful voices. Some have a keen sense of smell. What do you do well?

3. How would your life change if you lived in a wheelchair? If you only had one arm? If you couldn't see? If you couldn't hear or speak?

4. Make a list of all the physical resources that you have. How do these resources help you be successful?

CHAPTER 4

Hidden Rules Among Classes

For the third straight day, Carlos was late coming home from school. Pete decided it was better to ask than it was to worry. As Carlos turned the corner with his school books under one arm, Pete thought he looked more bewildered than upset. He gave Carlos a minute to drop his books on the step and settle down beside them. Then Pete asked quietly, "A little late from school again today?"

"Yep," Carlos replied.

"You're not having a problem with those big kids again, are you?"

"Nope."

"It's not after-school detention, is it?"

"Worse than that." Carlos gave a big sigh, then looked up at Pete and caught his good eye with a

puzzled expression. "I think I got me a job I can't quit!"

"Well, now how did _that_ happen?" asked Pete, smiling.

"On Monday, after lunch," Carlos began, "the teacher asked for a volunteer to help her. I thought I might get out of a little math to go and find the custodian or something, so I shot my hand up. She thanked me for being so enthusiastic and told me to wait after school. She would let me know then how I could help. After school, she had me carry some boxes for her from the back of the classroom to the storage room down the hall. Then she had me carry some more boxes from the storage room to the classroom. All the time I was working she was talking. She asked me a few questions, but mostly she talked about herself. And she talked a whole lot about her cat."

Still trying to read the look on Carlos' face, Pete asked, "Were the boxes heavy?"

"No, the work wasn't hard, and it wasn't too bad having to listen to her talk about her cat. But yesterday, during free reading time, she came by my desk and asked if I could help her again."

Pete smiled. "More boxes?"

"No, this time she wanted me to move some textbooks from the bookshelves into one of the closets. That wasn't too bad, but she talked again the whole time, and I don't really understand a lot of what she talks about."

"And today?"

"While she was passing out papers at the end of the day, she said she sure could use my help again this afternoon."

"And you stayed to help her..."

"She's a nice enough lady," Carlos said, "but I'm afraid I have me a job I can't quit."

"You know, I ran into a situation like this once, and it can be kind of tough." Pete tilted back in the straight-back kitchen chair that he had put out on the porch. Carlos leaned in, waiting for the story.

Cousin Jimmy's Dilemma

Back when I had a telephone, I picked it up one evening, and it was my Cousin Jimmy on the line. I could tell by the tone of his voice that he was troubled by something, and I wondered immediately if he were in jail again and needed me to spot his bail.

"Where are you calling from?" I asked.

"I'm at home," he answered, but I could still tell he had something on his mind. Maybe his car had been towed and he needed money to get it out of the impoundment lot. Before I could ask another question, he started in.

"I got myself into big trouble this time, and I really need your help. I think I got me a job I can't quit." Then he proceeded to tell me how he got into such a terrible predicament.

It seems he had been unemployed for a while and was in need of some cash. Besides, his mother had been riding him about getting a job and how his big brother Richard had a really good job. Richard had been working downtown at a construction site for more than a year as the

112

foreman's right-hand man. He seemed able to get work out of people when nobody else could and was really acting more like the boss than the boss himself. So Jimmy decided to see if Richard could get him on at the site.

Richard wasn't real keen on the idea, but since Jimmy was his brother, he went to his boss and asked if Jimmy could be hired. Jimmy started that afternoon, and it all went pretty well for a few months. The pay was good, and Jimmy caught up on all his debts. He was even able to buy his mother some things for the house. But, as the weather began to turn cold, so did Jimmy's attitude. The boss started wearing on his nerves, and he couldn't understand how his brother could have worked for the man as long as he had.

One cold morning Jimmy went in a little late. He didn't tell me so, but I imagine he went in late on purpose. When the boss began fussing at him, he and Jimmy got into a shouting match. Before it was over, Jimmy had gotten himself fired. The next morning, Jimmy stayed in his warm bed instead of getting up in the cold and going off to work. For the rest of the week, he stayed out late at night and slept until noon. On the following

Monday, his brother Richard woke him up at nine o'clock in the morning. Jimmy squinted at his brother and asked him why he wasn't down at work.

"You think I could work for that jerk after he fired you?" Richard answered. He went on to recount the many complaints Jimmy had lodged against their boss over the past months. He finished by strongly stating, "I just can't work for a man who would fire my brother."

Jimmy knew his brother wanted to work and needed the paycheck to support his family. The worst part about his brother being unemployed was that every morning at eight-thirty or nine o'clock, Richard came over to their mother's house. Jimmy slept on the couch in the living room, and there was no way he could get his sleep when Richard came over every morning for coffee and company. This went on for two or three weeks. One afternoon, while Richard was over at the unemployment office, the phone rang.

Jimmy's mother turned to him and said, "It's the boss from down at the construction site."

"Did you tell him Richard's not in?"

"He wants to talk to you."

Jimmy reluctantly took the phone, and the boss told him that work wasn't going very well since Richard left. They were behind schedule and were spending time on rebuilds that never would have happened if Richard were there. Jimmy thought the problem was simple enough to solve. Why didn't he just offer Richard his job back? Jimmy smiled to himself, then said, "You could give him a nice raise."

"I've already offered him his job back, with a nice raise. But he says he can't work for a man who fired his brother. That's why I'm calling you. I need you to come back to work for me. I'll even give you a raise. What do you say?"

What could Jimmy say? He didn't like the

man any more than he did the day he was fired. But he knew Richard needed the job, and the raise might make up for the time that Richard was out of work because of him. Richard was happy as could be when he found out that the boss had called Jimmy to offer him his job back. The following morning the brothers were back on the site.

"Two weeks later," Pete said, "I got the call from my Cousin Jimmy. 'I'm in big trouble,' he said. 'I think I got me a job I can't quit.'"

Pete let his chair come down with a thump. "Sounds to me like you got yourself one of those jobs like my Cousin Jimmy."

"So how did Jimmy get out of it?" Carlos asked.

"He had to wait until the building was finished. Then he could get his unemployment. When Richard went to work for the boss on the next site, Jimmy told him it was too far to drive. He wasn't going to get himself into another predicament."

"But school's not out for five more months," Carlos protested.

"Maybe you'll get lucky, and your teacher will have a meeting to go to tomorrow. In the meantime, ask her about her cat. That will keep her from asking you questions, and maybe her life will make more sense to you."

"People sure live funny," Carlos said, thinking about his teacher. "She said she drives an hour to get home each night, and when she gets there, it's just she and her cat. I wonder if lots of people live weird lives, or just teachers?"

Pete looked over at Carlos. "Back when I was in school all the teachers were just like our aunts and uncles. In fact, one of the teachers at my school <u>was</u> my aunt. It was a lot harder for kids back then, because your teachers could keep track of you in the evenings and on weekends. I had one teacher who used to ask me every week at Sunday school if I had finished my homework. When I got home from *church, my mama would make me sit down and do my work before I could go out and play. After our schools were shut down, our teachers were sent to other schools. That's when we ended up with teachers who would try to get to know us, but who could never understand."*

An Experiment in Distance Learning

Not so long ago, I read a story about a backwoods area in Arkansas. A few families lived way back in the hollows, and many days the roads were so bad a school bus couldn't drive back there and pick up the school children. For years and years they had a little one-room schoolhouse and a teacher who lived in the hollow with the families. Even though this was a bit old-fashioned, the families liked it, the teacher liked it, and the children seemed to learn what all the rest of the school kids learned.

A professor at the university in Fayetteville, who was doing research in what was called "distance learning," decided this little hollow was just distant enough to be part of his research. The professor convinced members of the state board of education that "distance learning" could save them money. Then he talked with the local school board about all the new lessons that could be beamed into the hollow on a satellite. Finally, he convinced a big communications com-

pany to provide the equipment. Before you knew it, every home up and down the hollow had a television set hooked up to one big satellite dish. A team of university students went from house to house showing the families how to tune in the lessons that were being beamed in from all over the world. By the time the college students left, the families liked it, the children liked it, and the school board liked it. The TV teachers didn't know whether they liked it or not because they didn't even know the students who were receiving the lessons being transmitted.

Satisfied with his work, the professor published a series of related articles and a textbook on distance learning, then moved to another university and decided to do research in a different area of technology. Several years later he found himself traveling through Arkansas and decided to wander back up into the hollow to see how modern technology had changed things. He was surprised to see that the satellite dish had been tipped over and wires strung to it so that it would support a large crop of bush beans. He also found a new corrugated tin shed that was stacked full of TV monitors. He noted that the old schoolhouse was once again open and saw the teacher working diligently to teach students of all ages.

The professor found a member of the local school board and argued passionately for the financial and educational benefits of learning by satellite. "Don't you realize," he said, "that the teachers on the satellite system know so many more lessons than the teacher you have down there at the schoolhouse?"

"Yes, we realize that," the board member replied. "But the teacher down at the schoolhouse knows us!"

"That's the way it used to be at our school-house," Pete said to Carlos. "Now we have teachers like your teacher. She's a good woman, and she seems to like you quite a bit."

"But she lives an hour away," Carlos added, "and she goes home every night to be with her cat."

Pete watched as Carlos put the finishing touches on his third poster. He kept going back into his little bag to find another broken crayon in order to add color. "So your teacher is having the kids in your class elect a President?"

Carlos grabbed another crayon and underlined the word <u>vote</u>. "With this upcoming primary election, our teacher said we should learn about politics and how it works. I tried to tell her that you told me politics didn't work, at least not in our neighborhood. But she's still making us have the election."

Pete looked at Carlos' posters and asked, "So,

aren't you running for office?"

"The teacher asked for volunteers, and I already knew what that meant. Besides, Darnell told me if I helped him get elected, he'd name me his Secretary of State. I think that's fancy language for calling me his right-hand man.

"Maybe this way," continued Carlos, "I can have an important job, and I'll only have to answer to one person. But Darnell will have all those people who voted for him wanting something in return for their votes."

"Sounds to me like you have it down," Pete said with a smile, "but you'd better be careful; this politics is a tricky business."

The Alley Cat's Secretary of State

Word spread through the neighborhood that Tom Cat, the king of the back alley, was looking for a Secretary of State. All the animals of the neighborhood were always trying to get on the alley cat's good side, but not so many were willing to come face to face and give it a try. On the designated day, only three showed up to apply for the job. Standing by the garbage cans were Rat, Squirrel, and Little Rabbit. Tom Cat, stretched out on top of one of the garbage cans, glared down on the three and asked why they had bothered his sleep. "We've come to apply for the job," Rat explained.

"You know, Secretary of State," Squirrel added.

Little Rabbit said nothing. He just looked down at the pavement wondering what had possessed him to come and apply for the job.

"It's true what you've heard—that I need a new Secretary of State," Cat said, stretching his claws and leaping down onto the pavement. "However, the one I select for the position must have a gift for saying the right thing at the right time. The last one to hold the job just didn't have that quality."

Rat looked at the other two and felt confident that he should have the job. Squirrel felt that such a skill could not be any harder than balancing on the telephone wire walking between poles. Little Rabbit stared at the pavement.

"I suppose we should have a little test," said Tom Cat. "The one who best answers my question will be given the job."

With that, Rat stepped forward confidently. Cat opened his mouth and exhaled in Rat's direction. "Tell me," the alley cat asked, "is my breath sweet, or is it not?"

The rat smelled every last bit of a three-day binge on the alley cat's breath and almost fainted from the odor. But Rat thought best not to tell the truth and replied, "My friend, I have never smelled such sweet breath. Such breath could compete with the smell of  baked bread that comes from the bakery when the wind blows up the alley from the west."

"Just as I thought," Tom Cat said. "You want only to flatter me. Such a speaker has no regard for the truth but cares only for his own well-being. I'm afraid you would be a danger to my political future." Whereupon the alley cat pounced on the rat and ate him.

Then he turned his attention to Squirrel.

Opening his mouth wide, the alley cat asked the question a second time: "Is my breath sweet, or is it not?"

Squirrel smelled the cat's foul breath but hesitated to answer. The cat showed its claws, so Squirrel cleared his little throat to give a reply.

"My friend, you will see that I will not ignore the facts in order to flatter you. You can always rely upon me for the truth. In fact, your breath smells worse than the smell of decomposing garbage that comes from the dump when the wind blows up the alley from the east."

"Just as I thought," the alley cat replied. "You are the kind of creature who speaks directly, without ever thinking about the feelings of others. That is the kind of assistant who creates arguments and bad feelings wherever he goes—and one who could ruin my political future." So the cat pounced on the squirrel and ate him, too.

As he finished eating, Tom Cat wiped his mouth and turned to Little Rabbit. "Now it's your turn. Is my breath sweet, as Rat claimed, or is it foul, as Squirrel described?" He opened his mouth and blew a breath toward the trembling rabbit.

"Well?" the alley cat asked, moving in a

little closer. "What is it? Sweet or foul?"

The little rabbit raised his head, his nose twitching uncontrollably. In a small voice he stated, "My friend, your question comes at a most unfortunate time."

"What's the trouble?" asked Tom Cat, slightly annoyed.

"I have a terrible cold," the rabbit replied, his nose twitching even more. "I really can't smell a thing one way or the other."

With that, the cat smiled. "My main man!" he declared. "You are the one for the job. For an ordinary creature, a sense of smell is important. But those who enter politics are better off without one."

And so Little Rabbit became the alley cat's Secretary of State, and he still is, if I'm not mistaken. Each and every day he twitches his nose to show Tom Cat that he still has a cold and can't smell a thing one way or the other.

"I didn't know the animals in the neighborhood were so deeply involved in politics," Carlos said, *smiling up at Pete.*

Pete nodded toward a few dogs that were sniffing each other in the lot across from the church. "It's not just the alley cat," he said. "Once upon a time the dogs decided they needed a President, but they weren't sure how to go about it. One dog nominated a bulldog because he was the strongest. Of course, another objected, saying the bulldog was too slow and too stupid. That dog nominated a greyhound because it was the fastest of the dogs. But others complained because the greyhound not only couldn't fight, he didn't even have a bark. Finally, one dog suggested they elect the dog that smelled the best underneath its tail. Well, that seemed reasonable enough, but you can see by those mutts in the lot over there that the dogs are still trying to find their leader."

127

Pete looked back at Carlos, who glanced at his watch for the third time in five minutes. "Do you have some place you have to be?" Pete inquired.

"Mama wants me home by four o'clock. She's going to take me to Shoe Mart to buy me a new pair of dress shoes."

"What's the occasion?"

"I'm not sure it is an occasion," Carlos answered. "It's some sort of party at Mrs. Steinberg's house. Mama has been working for Mr. and Mrs. Steinberg for four or five years now. This weekend they're having some kind of celebration. I think they've been together for fifty years or something. Their kids are throwing them a party and they invited Mama and me to come. Mama said she would just as soon come late and clean up, but Mrs. Steinberg's son said he was paying someone else to do that. He just wanted Mama to be there to help them celebrate. I think Mama is going to have to work four more years to pay for her new dress and my shoes. Mama is a little nervous about the whole deal. That's why I keep checking my watch. I want to be home on time, but I don't want to be early. If we have time to spare, Mama will start asking, 'Do you think my dress is the right color?'"

Carlos looked up at Pete, who had taken in the entire explanation with an expanding smile creasing his face.

"How am I supposed to act when I get to this party?" Carlos asked.

"If I had asked myself that question a few years ago, it would have saved me a huge dry-cleaning bill."

Carlos looked at his watch to make sure he would have time for Pete's story.

"What time is it?" Pete asked.

"Ten 'til four."

"I can tell you this story in ten minutes."

A Vest Pocket Full of Beef

Several years ago, a politician in town was campaigning to be re-elected mayor. He decided he was going to have a big dinner and invite one or two prominent citizens from each neighborhood in town. Perhaps he had heard I was good for a story or two. Maybe he heard the reputation I had in this neighborhood was a good one. Or maybe he just felt like a man with one eye would not be able to see through his election promises. At any rate, he invited me and Reverend Johnson to come represent our neighborhood at his big dinner.

The Saturday of the party arrived, but I wasn't sure I was going to be able to attend. Miss Wilson, over on Daniel Street, had been filling up buckets in her living room every time it rained, and I had promised to help put a new roof on her house the first time we had some good weather. I was hammering shingles when Reverend Johnson came by to pick me up. He was all decked out in his Sunday preaching clothes. He took a look at my sweaty clothes and was pleased to hear me say that if I made it to the party I would go by myself a little later.

I finished the job and climbed down the ladder. Miss Wilson offered to feed me beans and rice for dinner, but I told her I thought I'd mosey on over to the big party and get something to eat

 there. As late as it was, I decided not to stop by the house and change. I just cleaned up a little with the hose in Miss Wilson's backyard. When I got to the party, I was stopped on the front walk. An off-duty deputy explained to me this was a private party, and I could not just walk in off the street. I explained I had an invitation and was not just walking in off the street, but had come down from Miss Wilson's roof in order to attend. The deputy took a long look at my overalls and my work boots and was unconvinced. Turned away, I went back to the house and changed into my finest three-piece suit. I even put on my black-velvet eye patch.

The second time I approached the party, it was obvious by the deputy's reaction that now I truly belonged. When I walked by him, he took

a long look at me, trying to figure out if he had seen me somewhere before. As soon as I walked through the door, the host spotted me and had me escorted to a place of honor at the head table. I believe Reverend Johnson would have gladly traded the opportunity to offer the invocation for my chair at the head table. A waiter brought me a big plate of barbecue with a side of potato salad and beans.

I was hungry enough to eat two platefuls and, looking around the table, I surmised that going back for seconds would be acceptable behavior. At the same time I was looking at the plates of food, I also took a look at the faces of the men who were eating. All around that table were government folks who had promised to pave neighborhood streets with gold. I wasn't sure about the other folks' neighborhoods, but I knew that around here we can't even get the potholes filled. I waited until our host was finished with a conversation and had turned to admire my velvet eye patch.

Just at that moment, I took a big forkful of potato salad and—very deliberately—spread it on the sleeve of my suit jacket from my elbow to my shoulder. While I had his attention, I took a spoonful of beans and poured them into my pant cuff. Then I stood up, grabbed my watch chain, and pulled my watch out of my vest pocket. With one hand I checked the time, and with the other I slid a slice of beef, dripping with barbecue sauce, right into my vest pocket. Being in politics, our host had seen some rather bizarre behavior in his time. Eventually, he was able to force a smile and ask for an explanation.

"I came earlier and neither my good stories nor my good name—nor my word that I had an invitation—could get me past the sidewalk," I stated. "I later returned, the same man but dressed in fine clothes. It was the clothes that got me into the feast, so I assumed it was the clothes that should be fed."

I decided my dinner would be more satisfying if I took up Miss Wilson's offer of beans and rice. As she and I were finishing, Reverend Johnson stopped by on his way home from the party. He couldn't help commenting on my poor display of manners: "If only you would learn to flatter the mayor and act subservient as I do, you would not have to live on beans and rice."

I winked at Miss Wilson and replied, "If only you would learn to live on beans and rice, you would not have to flatter the mayor and act subservient."

"As for you, Carlos, it's four o'clock, so you'd best be getting home. I don't believe Mr. and Mrs. Steinberg are running for election. They probably just want you and your mama to go to the party and have a nice time. So act like you're having fun—and eat a piece of cake for me."

Carlos stood up and headed home. "I'm sure it will be a great party," he called over his shoulder.

Pete watched his young friend head down the street. Any two people who can live together for fifty years, thought Pete, deserve a great party. Either that, or they need their heads examined.

QUESTIONS: CHAPTER 4
Hidden Rules Among Classes

Cousin Jimmy's Dilemma

1. Hidden rules are those unspoken cues that people use to let other people know whether they do or do not belong to the group. What are the hidden rules among your group of friends? How do you know whether people do or do not belong to your group?

2. In the story, Richard keeps working even though he doesn't like the boss. Jimmy, however, quits. What are the hidden rules that Jimmy is following?

3. Why do people quit a job because they don't "like" the boss?

4. Why do students quit working in school when they don't like a teacher? Is it possible to not like someone but still work for him or her?

5. Is it honest to work for someone you don't like?

6. Why did Richard quit the job after Jimmy did? Why do people "defend their own" even when they don't agree with them? Why did Jimmy go back to work? What hidden rule was Jimmy following? If you were Jimmy, what would you have done? If you were Richard, what would you have done?

7. For some individuals, things are possessions. For some, people are possessions. If you spend your money on a house, car, and education, then work and achievement tend to be very important to you. If you spend your money on fun, entertainment, and staying alive, then people tend to be very important to you. What is important to you?

An Experiment in Distance Learning

1. Why can things never take the place of relationships?

2. In what ways can knowledge and achievement harm a relationship? In what ways can distance change a relationship?

3. Can relationships harm achievement? If so, how?

4. When two people have a good relationship, there is mutual respect. What is mutual respect?

Alley Cat's Secretary of State

1. There are hidden rules in what one person can say to another and be safe. In this story, Tom Cat wants a helper who will always say the right thing. Do you trust people who flatter you? Are they trying to cheat you? Or are they trying to be pleasant? Do you trust people who <u>always</u> tell it like it is? Is that a good thing to do?

2. The rabbit neither flatters nor confronts. He avoids the issue. Is that a good thing to do?

3. It is often said that a person can flee, fight, or flow. Which of these would you do first? Why?

4. In the hidden rules of different groups, some groups think it's better to be a rabbit. Some believe it's better to be a rat. Some believe it's better to be a squirrel. What do you believe?

5. If you are a person who fights first, how does that help you? How does it hurt you? If you are a person who flees (runs) first, how does that help you? How does it hurt you?
If you are a person who flows (goes with whatever is happening), how does that help you? How does it hurt you?

6. Does the group you are in think it's better to fight, to flee, or to flow?

A Vest Pocket Full of Beef

1. Why does the preacher follow the hidden rules the mayor uses? Why does Pete follow a different set of hidden rules?

2. Pete thinks people should be recognized for who they are. The preacher thinks people should be recognized for the way they are dressed and the way they act. Who is right? Are they both right?

3. What are the hidden rules in your group? Are there certain ways to dress and behave that tell other people you belong to that group?

4. If you want to make money by having a good-paying job, what are the hidden rules about dress and behavior that you must follow? How do you feel about those rules?

5. At the end of the story, the preacher says, "If only you would learn to flatter the mayor ... you would not have to live on beans and rice." Pete replies, "If only you would learn to live on beans and rice, you wouldn't have to flatter the mayor and act subservient." What does this mean? Which one would you do and why?

CHAPTER 5

Spring Break:
A Leisurely Look at the Characteristics of Generational Poverty

Carlos knew being out of school for spring break was a mixed blessing. On the one hand, there was no homework, no teachers fussing at him because his mama didn't sign a paper with a bad grade, and he could do pretty much what he wanted. On the other hand, he would have to settle for a lot less breakfast and lunch, and there was no one to stop the seventh-graders from chasing him through the neighborhood and demanding his quarters.

By late afternoon on the first day of vacation, Carlos was at the wrong end of a chase when he zipped around the corner and found Pete sitting on the step. Relieved, he sat down next to him, knowing the chasers wouldn't bother him here.

"Where are you going in such a hurry?" Pete asked, expecting to get only part of the story.

"I was hoping to get home before Mama. She told me to stay in the house all day, but she doesn't realize how boring it is. I was going to get back in time, but I kind of got sidetracked on the way home." He looked up the street and saw his front door was open, a signal he was too late to avoid a whipping.

"I suppose there's no hurry now," continued Carlos with a sigh. "She's going to need time to find the belt. One of these days I'm just not going home. She probably wouldn't even care."

"I imagine there might be some who wouldn't care," replied Pete, "but I don't think it would be your mama."

The Woman in the Blue House on Oak Street

Some years ago, there was a woman who lived in that blue house on the corner of Oak and Nataly. She had two boys. The older boy was very respectful and very responsible and looked out

140

for his mama all the time. He was also a hard worker and never missed a day of school. When he got out of high school he had a scholarship to go away to college, but he was only gone for about six weeks. He missed his mother, and he knew she needed him, so he left school and came back home. He got a job at the refinery and moved back into the house to keep it up and take care of his mother.

The second son was very different from his brother. The younger boy loved a good time and worried his mama to death. He couldn't keep a job, so he was always borrowing money from his mother. That is what she called it, "borrowing." The older boy knew that his brother took what he wanted and thought nothing of it.

The younger son, though perhaps smarter in school than his older brother, seldom studied, so he didn't earn a scholarship to college. In fact, he didn't even finish high school. After he dropped out, he worked the club scene as a drummer and a bouncer and, some say, as a drunk and a drug pusher. When he finally left town to go up north, it broke his mother's heart. His older brother, on the other hand, was very glad his brother (and his strange friends) would no longer be hanging around the blue house on Oak Street.

The older brother was not nearly so happy, however, when he found out that the younger son had taken his mother's Social Security check, as well as her only valuable jewelry: a diamond bracelet and earrings.

When the younger son hit the big city, he thought he had died and gone to heaven. He bought some hot new clothes and began working with the best bands in town. He usually didn't see the light of day, but worked and played from sunset to sunrise. He got a fancy car and was always surrounded by beautiful women. If he had money, he spent it. "That's what money is for," he said, flashing a fat roll of bills. If he didn't have money, he hung around with people who did.

Over time, however, the night life and the drinking took their toll and, eventually, the younger son came to ruin. His skills diminished and so did his circle of friends. He would show up for a gig but couldn't keep up. Then he started not showing up at all, and he began to fall through the cracks of life. While he experimented with drugs, he never became an addict. On the steep slide to the bottom, though, he eased his suffering by turning more and more to the bottle.

Finally, he found himself on the street, sleeping on sidewalks and under railroad bridges. He searched for food in garbage cans and begged for money on the street corner. Like many other street people, he spent the money he got, not on nourishment to feed the body, but on liquor to numb the soul. There was never enough in any bottle, however, to drown his suffering.

Early one morning, the young man sat huddled on a radiator grate—hungry, freezing, and not caring about either. He emptied the last of his bottle and rolled it into the gutter. He put his head back against the cold stone of the office building behind him and closed his eyes. Two men passed him on the sidewalk on their way to work, one telling the other what he had bought for his mother for Christmas. At the thought of his own mother, the younger son began to cry. Then he began to think. On Oak Street he always had food to eat. His mother always made sure he had a place to sleep. If he went back home, he could keep up the yard for his meals. Even if he went back home, and she wouldn't allow him inside the house but let him sleep on the porch, it would be warmer and safer than where he was sleeping now.

Somehow, he found the strength and the means to make his way back home to his neighborhood. All the way home, he planned his speech. He would beg his mama for forgiveness. He would promise to make it up to her, to pay for the jewelry and earn back the money he stole from her. He would tell her he was willing to sleep on

 the porch and work around the house for his food. When he arrived, it was with the greatest dread that he stood and looked at the blue house on the corner of Oak and Nataly. Twice he turned and walked away. Twice he returned to gaze up at the porch and the front door.

Finally, he approached the house, walked up the steps onto the porch, and knocked at the

door. His mother answered the door. The moment he began to speak, before he could ask for forgiveness, before he could explain himself, before he could promise to change, she flung open the door, threw her arms around him, and began to cry. A voice from the back of the house called out, "Who is it, Mama?"

When she didn't answer, the older son came to the door to see who was there. He was not nearly so overjoyed to see who had arrived on Christmas Eve. He was even more unhappy when his brother sat in the place of honor at dinnertime. And he was flat-out steamed when his mother gave the returning son not the guest room but the best room.

Late in the afternoon on Christmas day, when the new arrival was asleep on the couch, the older brother stood with his mother at the kitchen sink and complained bitterly about his brother's return. His brother had left and never written. He had stolen the jewelry and the money. He was less than nothing.

"Oh, no," the mother replied. "He is more than nothing. He is flesh and blood. Just like you, he still looks like he was spit right out of my mouth. Now he has come home. The greatest gift a mother could have at Christmas is to have all her children under the same roof."

"You need to get on home, too," Pete said. "If you don't put up too much of a fuss when your mama finds that belt, you may find that your mama won't put too much energy into her part either."

But Carlos wasn't thinking about the belt; he was still thinking about the story.

"It seems I've heard that story somewhere before," he said, looking puzzled.

"If you keep going to church with your mama," Pete said with a smile, "I imagine you'll hear it sometime again."

"Where are you heading off to this morning?" Pete asked from the doorway as Carlos hustled by with his head down. Carlos mumbled a response. "How's that?" Pete questioned, raising his chin and squinting.

Carlos came back to the step and answered, "I was heading down to the creek to meet Seth and Terry."

"I thought your mama didn't want you down at the creek." Pete leaned against the wrought-iron railing and loomed over Carlos. "Don't I recall you telling me your mama doesn't want you running with Seth and Terry? Is your mama home?"

"No," Carlos answered, still not ready to sit down. "She's over cleaning at Miss Emma's house."

"Just because she's cleaning doesn't mean she's too busy to worry. She's expecting you to stay clear of trouble." Pete lowered himself onto the step, his feet, at the end of those long legs, settling on the sidewalk. "Have a seat before the Devil hauls you away."

Little Eight John

A family who used to live next door to Miss Emma had a whole brood of boys. They named the first boy John, after his father. Everybody called that child Junior. They named the second boy John, after his father, and everybody called that child Trey. They had five more boys, and they named them all John, after their father. Those boys had nicknames, too: Red and Bubba, Gordie and Slim, and one called Mohammed. I can't remember which was which. After their eighth boy, they quit. The last one they called Little Eight John. He was named after his brothers.

Most of those boys were good boys and didn't worry their mother. But Little Eight John was bad to the bone. If his mama told him to do one thing, he would do just the opposite and then think it was funny! If his mama told him not to step on the toads because it would bring bad luck to the family, he would race out the door and stomp those little toads flat, all the while laughing at his own mischief.

When the car wouldn't start, or the TV went out, the family blamed Little Eight John because of the toad squashing. He just laughed and laughed. His mama would say, "Little Eight John, don't sit backwards in your chair; it will bring troubles down on this household." Little Eight

John would sit backwards in every chair in the house. In the after-noon, when the cornbread burned and the beans got scorched, everyone knew it was Eight John's fault. Little Eight John thought it was hysterical.

TEE HEE

If you think Little Eight John was bad at home, you should have seen him at school. He ran in the halls, he talked without raising his hand, he sneaked food into class, and he never did his homework. He laughed at the teacher when she corrected him and told the principal the pops he gave didn't hurt a bit.

"You might as well give me two more," he said in the office. "It will save you the trouble the next time I come down."

He was so bad, they stuck him away in one of those special-behavior classes before he fin-ished first grade. Even then, some days he got suspended and had to stay home and worry his mama.

"Don't count your teeth," his mother told

Eight John, "or a sickness will come on your family." But Little Eight John went right ahead and counted his uppers and his lowers. He counted his teeth every day, once with his finger and once with his tongue. When his mama got migraine headaches and his brother Bubba got fever, Little Eight John got the giggles.

I mean to tell you, this boy was rotten. His mother would warn him, "Don't sleep with your head at the foot of the bed or you will bring the weary-money blues right into this house." So Little Eight John slept with his head at the foot of every bed in the house. Sure enough, late in the month someone robbed Little Eight John's mama, and she didn't have enough money to pay the water bill. Little Eight John thought it was funny when the water got cut off. He liked being dirty.

It got so bad that Little Eight John wouldn't even behave in church. On Sunday mornings he moaned and groaned about the length of the sermon and the choice of the songs. One Sunday he was caught stealing money from the offering plate. His mama pleaded with him to be good.

"If you don't mend your ways, the Devil himself is going to come after you."

Little Eight John didn't listen to one thing his mother said. One Sunday morning, after pretending to be deathly ill and unable to attend church, he was home alone playing, and the Devil did come after Little Eight John. He caught Little Eight John standing on the kitchen table and turned him into a grease spot right there next to the burn mark from the iron.

That was the end of Little Eight John, and that's what happens to children who don't mind what their mamas say. At least that's what Little Eight John's mama told his seven surviving brothers after prayer at Sunday dinner.

"I understand his family couldn't bear to look at that grease spot," Pete said, "so they sold the kitchen table at a yard sale. In fact, Miss Emma bought that table. It's the one that's in her kitchen now."

Carlos smiled at Pete and thanked him for the story.

"Where are you headed?" Pete asked as Carlos stood up and turned to walk away.

"I thought I might run over to Miss Emma's

house," Carlos called over his shoulder, "and see if Mama needs any help cleaning."

The next morning Carlos went by Pete's empty step and walked the three blocks to the park. Just as he guessed, when he approached the park he saw Pete sitting on one of the park benches looking out across a playing field toward the bay. Carlos walked up quietly and slipped onto one end of the bench.

"Still on vacation?"

"Sure am. For a whole week. I don't have to do anything ... Besides, there's nothing to do."

"Just because school is out doesn't mean you can stop thinking. When school's out, you need to think even more. Otherwise, you really won't have anything to do all week."

"I don't see what you mean," said Carlos.

"Close your eyes. Can you see yourself sitting on this bench?"

"Yes."

152

"Now, can you see yourself sitting on this bench for a week?"

"Hmmm ... Only if you tell stories all day."

The Eagle Chick

There once was a man who went down to the zoo at night and stole an eagle's egg. He came home and put that egg in the nest of a hen he kept in his backyard. Sure enough, when that chicken hatched its eggs, there was an eaglet right in the middle of a dozen chicks.

The eaglet grew up with those chicks and learned to do just what they did. He scratched for earthworms and other bugs in the backyard. He clucked, and he cackled. From time to time he would thrash his wings and fly a few feet from one side of that backyard to the other. You see, he thought he was a chicken and never imagined he was anything else.

Years went by, and chickens came and went in that man's backyard, but the eagle stayed because he was a source of amusement to the man and his neighbors. The man couldn't imagine eating him for dinner like he did the chickens.

One afternoon, when the eagle was quite old, he looked up and saw a magnificent bird far above him in the cloud-less sky. It glided gracefully in a majes-tic manner way up among the high and powerful

wind currents, with scarcely a beat of its strong golden wings. The eagle stared at the awesome sight.

"Who's that?" he asked.

"That's the eagle, the king of the birds," answered one of the chickens in the backyard. "He belongs to the sky. We belong to the earth— we are chickens."

They both went back to scratching in the dirt for bugs.

That old eagle lived and died a chicken, because that's what he thought he was.

"Do you remember when you told me you failed that reading project because you didn't have any of that big drawing paper at your house the teacher wanted you to use?" Pete asked.

"Yeah, I remember."

"Do you remember when you got a bad grade on that science project because your mama was sick and couldn't take you to the library?"

"I remember," Carlos answered, closing his eyes and wincing a little bit.

"Well, you better close your eyes and see if you can't imagine yourself doing something besides sitting here on this bench for the next week. Because it's your spring break, and if you fail this time, it will be a failure of the imagination."

Carlos kept his eyes closed for a long time, then smiled and opened them back up. "I'm going to go play now," Carlos said. "Maybe you can just sit here and think of a story to tell me this afternoon."

Pete watched him race across the park toward the bay. He looked up in the sky for eagles and let *the sunlight wash his face.*

Pete was sitting on the park bench. Carlos came up and flopped down on the other end. "When you were little, did you ever wonder what you were going to do when you grew up?"

"What makes you think I was ever little?" Pete asked with a grin. "To be honest, I never had a time like spring break to think much about it. I was always helping my daddy or my uncle in the fields. My mama used to say that idle hands were the Devil's playground."

"My mama says I shouldn't worry about what I will do when I grow up," said Carlos. "She says God will take care of me, and He can worry about my destiny."

"I suppose your mama is right about God looking after you. But I don't think He will get upset if you keep an active hand in your own destiny."

In Whose Hands Is the Fate of the Army?

When this land right here belonged to Spain, there was a General who led his army on a campaign across the countryside. Day after day he led his troops into battle, and day after day they were victorious. He captured one town after another and, finally, neared a large city by the coast. At that point his troops were tired of battle and a long way from home. The General wanted to press on and capture the last city, but he and the troops knew it was defended by a well-armed force, twice the number of his men. Even so, the General felt certain his army could win, though his soldiers were reluctant.

Early in the morning, after his men were well-rested, he called them onto the hillside where he had built a small altar. He stood before them, asking in prayer for advice from the Almighty. At the end of the ceremony, the troops raised their heads from prayer and watched as the General fished a large gold coin from his pocket. The early-morning sun glinted off the coin as the General raised it over his head.

"I will toss the coin to see how God directs us. If it comes up heads, we will win a great victory."

The soldiers watched in anticipation as the coin flew up into the air and tumbled back down onto the ground in front of the altar. The General bent down to pick it up, then raised it high for the soldiers to see.

The toss was indeed heads and, inspired by this holy sign, the soldiers pressed forward to easily overrun the city.

After the battle, a soldier said to the General, "When we have been shown that God is with us, nothing can challenge our destiny."

The General agreed with a serious nod. When the soldier had left, he again dug the gold coin out of his pocket and looked at the head of a king, engraved on both sides. He flipped the coin into the air, deftly caught it on its tumbling descent, and slipped it back into his pocket.

"Destiny indeed," he whispered, smiling ever so slightly.

"My mama not only believed that idle hands were the Devil's playground," said Pete, "she also believed that God helps those who help themselves. It won't hurt if you keep your mind busy wondering about what you're going to do when you grow up."

᠎ ᠎ ᠎ ᠎ ᠎ ᠎ ᠎ ᠎

"I want to believe that I can make things different," Carlos commented while sharing his sandwich with Pete, "but there always seems to be something standing in my way."

"If you want something badly enough, you just might have to shove that thing out of your way."

"That's easier said than done," Carlos replied , a bit of tuna <u>and</u> sarcasm on his tongue.

"You'd be surprised," Pete responded, wiping sandwich spread from the corner of his mouth with a red bandana.

The Story of Coach 'Stump' Barnes

When I was in high school, I had a class-mate named Benny Barnes. Benny was a couple of years older than I was. He was a senior when I was a sophomore. The reason I knew Benny was the same reason everybody knew Benny. He was a great athlete. He played on the football team and ran track, but he *was* the basketball team. In his junior year, Benny had been named second team all-state. He was such a natural. Folks said he must have been born with a basketball in his hand. He was about six feet tall, which was pretty tall back then, and slim-built. He was probably the closest thing to a Michael Jordan this city has ever seen.

Benny Barnes was not only great on the basketball court, he also was pretty good in the classroom. His mother was a smart lady but had never finished high school. She wanted nothing more than for Benny to get an education so he could take care of himself. Don't get me wrong, she was proud of what Benny could do on the football field and the basketball court, but her main concern was what he did in the classroom.

By the time Benny had finished his junior

year, a few of the colleges were beginning to send scouts to watch him play. I remember when a couple of scouts from the big universities stood out in the crowd. Everybody knew they had come to watch Benny, and most folks hoped Benny would choose to go to one of the smaller schools. The truth of the matter was, it was Benny's mama who would do the choosing when the time came.

Obviously, something must have happened, or everybody would know who Benny Barnes was, and I wouldn't have to be telling you this story. One afternoon after practice, Benny was on his way home with his books and his basketball. During the season, Benny always had a ball in his hand. He was dribbling the ball and looking straight ahead. In order to get over to the Tree streets where he lived, he had to cross the railroad tracks. Since he was working on his dribbling, he usually walked all the way down to the crossing, though it was a little farther to get home that way. Some of the other kids had decided to cross over, and a few always walked down the track.

On this particular afternoon, there were two boys walking down the tracks parallel to

161

Benny and headed in the same direction. I suppose he saw them but really didn't pay any attention until he heard the train whistle blow. At first he thought the boys were playing chicken. He used to do that himself before his mama caught him and took the belt to his rear end. Finally, he realized that the boy on the track wanted to get off; he just couldn't. Benny dropped his books and ball and sprinted toward the railroad tracks. Sure enough, the boy had somehow caught his shoe in one of the rails and couldn't move. The train was getting louder and louder and, eventually, the sound of the train engine and the metal screeching of the brakes added to the boys' shouts and made the whole scene an incredible jumble of noise and fear.

Benny tugged and tugged on the boy's foot and, at the last second, managed to free it from the rail. The two of them fell to the side of the track, and the boy, though frightened to death, was unhurt. When Benny tried to get up, he had a funny feeling in his left leg. He looked down and saw that it was worse than a funny feeling. His leg was missing from the knee down.

By that time the train had stopped and

people were running from every direction. Eventually, Doc Johnson arrived, and Benny went to the hospital. I think Benny's mama was hospitalized for a while, too. Some folks said that Benny's mama suffered more at the loss of that leg than Benny did. He got better, and the doctors fixed him up with a wooden leg. At first it was just a wooden peg, like the pirates had, but eventually someone donated some money and sent him to a hospital where he could get fitted with a leg that looked more real. But even that leg with the hand-carved foot couldn't hide Benny's limp. It couldn't get him back on the basketball court either. Worse than that to Benny's mother, Benny never showed up in the classroom again.

Over time, Benny left the neighborhood, and stories came back about drinking and drugs and trouble with the law. It always sounded worse than it really was, and no one ever talked bad about Benny himself. When Benny's mama left the neighborhood a couple of years after the accident, the only time Benny's name was ever mentioned was when an up-and-coming ballplayer did something exciting. Then folks would say he was a regular Benny Barnes.

About four years ago Mr. Woodson, down at the barbershop, got a letter from his cousin in St. Louis. In the letter there was a news clipping about the Missouri state championship high school basketball team. The article talked about how the team  had been in the state finals three of the last five years and had won twice. The coach, when asked about the team's success, said, "If you want something badly enough, and are willing to work for it, you can accomplish lots more than a state championship."

The story also had a picture and caption: "Coach 'Stump' Barnes with State Championship Squad." There was a short paragraph in the story about the coach. It seemed Coach Barnes had lost part of a leg in an accident that ended his playing career, but had gone to school to become a teacher and later returned to his favorite pastime—basketball.

When Pete finished telling the story, there was a faraway look in his one eye. It made Carlos hurt to gaze at it. "You ever talk with Coach Barnes?" Carlos asked, hoping to distract Pete from his thought.

"I haven't talked with Benny in years," Pete answered without looking.

"Well, you sure know a lot about the man."

"I ought to. I'm the boy who had his foot stuck on the railroad track."

"There are times when I make up my mind that things are going to be different, and I work really hard," Carlos commented as he and Pete walked home from the park in the fading afternoon light. "But in the end, no matter how hard I try, things turn out the same."

"Isn't that the truth?" Pete agreed. "Sometimes that's just the way life is."

Looking for Paradise

He's in jail now, but I knew a man once who had just about all he could take. He had married badly for a third time, and the woman just would not quit nagging him. The kids from his first marriage came around always wanting money. The kids from his second marriage always wanted to sleep on the couch, then stole money from his wallet while he was out in the yard. He had to keep quitting his jobs because his car was either breaking down or being repossessed. His dog bit him and then ran away.

One day as he was walking down to the unemployment office, he saw his dog sitting in the shade of a big tree in a large fenced yard. The dog had a bone in his mouth. When the man called him to come over to the fence, the dog just looked up from the bone and growled. He thought about that dog the rest of the day and finally decided that maybe his dog was the smartest one of all.

Early the next morning the man left his sleeping wife in the bedroom and a grown son snoring on the couch in the front room. He stepped out onto the little porch, let the sagging screen door slam shut, and walked across the yard, stepping over the rusty chain that used to tether his dog. Up the street he headed, past the clinic, over the railroad tracks, behind the gas station, and out onto the highway.

This man had heard stories for years that, if one were to head south out of the city and travel two days, one would come to the town of Paradise. Folks talked about Paradise with tears in their eyes, cursing the day they had left, believing that the big city would be more exciting or more profitable. There were stories of others who left the big city never to return, and it was said these wise people had found true happiness in Paradise. Going up over a rise and leaving the city behind, the man headed south down the highway in the early-morning sun, determined to find Paradise and change his life.

All day he was on the road, hitching rides from town to town. A couple of times he got stuck and had to walk a few miles before he caught another ride. By the end of the day, he had put some miles between himself and his miserable existence. Wanting to find a place to spend the night, he left the highway. Underneath a bridge where a creek quietly ran toward the sea, he found a secluded spot. For supper, he heated up a can of beans on a little wood fire. After he ate, he got ready to go to sleep. Before he lay down to rest his head on his little sack of belongings, he took off his shoes and carefully placed them between himself and the creek bed, being certain to point them in the direction of Paradise, where he would be headed the next morning.

He went to sleep and dreamt dreams of a new and wonderful life. While he slept, a coyote snuck over the embankment and crept down to the water for a drink. As he crossed near the sleeping man, he warily sniffed the man's shoes, then slipped by to the water's edge. The coyote had just quenched his thirst when he was startled by the man's sudden and loud snore. Quickly, the animal scampered up the embankment, scrambling over those same shoes. The man didn't wake up and so failed to see the shoes flip over and come to rest pointing in the opposite direction.

The next morning the man awoke early, gathered up his belongings, and put on his shoes. He headed off in the direciton the shoes were pointing, happy with the thought that by day's end he would be in Paradise.

All day he hitched rides on the highway. Sometimes he had to walk a few miles before another car stopped to pick him up. Although he was quite weary by the end of the day, he was not too tired to feel the excitement of the great possiblilities that lay ahead. As evening came and the first stars appeared in the sky, the man came over a rise and looked down on the lights of what certainly must be Paradise.

It was a little bigger than he had expected and, as he headed into the center, it looked vaguely familiar. He cut behind a gas station, went over some railroad tracks, and at a corner where there was a building that looked like a clinic, he turned and went into a neighborhood. After walking a couple of blocks, he stopped in front of a little house with a rusty chain lying in the front yard. He stepped over the chain, climbed up the steps to the porch, and stood for a minute staring at the sagging screen door. "It looks a lot like my old house in that other city," he thought. But convinced that he was now in Paradise and certain that life would be better, he reached for the handle and opened the door.

Of course, everybody knows you just can't go walking into a stranger's house. Before he could even explain his presence in Paradise, a woman who looked just like his third wife grabbed the phone and called the police, while a man he didn't know pointed a gun at his chest.

The police came and took him to jail. It's not Paradise, but he does get three meals a day, and there's no one there who nags him or takes his money.

"It just goes to show," Pete said, stretching and rising to his feet, "that the changes you want to make don't always turn out the way you plan them. While you're sleeping, there are other folks who might stumble over your ideas."

"That's just it," Carlos said. "I have all kinds of things I want to do, but there's always somebody—

like Mama, or my teacher, or some big kids—or some reason why I can't do the things I want."

Pete looked up at the clouds. A bird was resting on a telephone wire. "That's a painful thing, knowing we all have a world we want to run and realizing there's only one world, and we all have to share it."

A Bird in the Hand

You remember Mr. P.G. Green, the old man who lived by himself in that little house on the corner of Ella and Hawthorne? He was the principal of the high school before they closed it down in 1969. He and his wife never had any kids. When she died, he was left by hiimself. He seemed to manage pretty well because he had all those kids up at the school. But when the high school was closed and he retired, all that was left for him was his garden.

Not that he still wasn't the topic of many conversations. Every time a school year started, parents would remember P.G. Green and tell stories about how smart he was. They'd tell their children about how he always seemed to know when kids were fixing to get into trouble. They told about how he would walk the streets late at night, grabbing kids who were up to no good and dragging them home to their parents. On and on the stories would go about Mr. P.G. Green, a man of great wisdom and caring.

One year, after school started, there were a couple of smart alecks who had skipped class and were hanging around the neighborhood. These young boys weren't hurting for brains, they just weren't putting the brains they had to any good use. As they sat on the curb sharing a cigarette, they commented on P.G. Green and how tired they were of hearing about how smart he was.

"He may have been smart once, but now he's just old," one said.

"I'll bet he never was as smart as folks say. And I'll bet he isn't half as smart as you or me," the other replied.

As they sat on the curb, they wished they could show the old man up and prove they were smarter than even P.G. Green. Then maybe everyone would see that they didn't need to be in school anymore.

The two boys went around to the back of a church where they had seen a bird flying into the eaves with a worm in its beak. Sure enough, they found a nest with baby birds. The next time the mother was off looking for more food, they snatched a baby bird out of the nest. Cupping it in their hands, they planned their trick. They were going to ask Mr. Green if the bird they held in their hand was dead or alive. If he said it was dead, they were going to open their hands and show him his mistake. If he said it was alive, they would snap the bird's neck and then reveal the  evidence to the contrary. Either way, they would be right, and the wise and famous P.G. Green would look the fool.

As they approached the little house on the corner of Ella and Hawthorne, Mr. Green looked up from his work in the flower garden.

"Shouldn't you boys be in school?" he asked. "Do your mamas know you aren't in class?"

"Don't worry about what our mamas

know," said one of the boys. "We want to see what you know."

Thrusting his hands out in front of him, the boy with the bird asked, "If you're so smart, tell us whether the bird I have in my hands is dead or alive."

Mr. P.G. Green looked long and hard at the two boys. He had spent thirty years working with boys just like these two. He quickly figured out exactly what they had on their minds. If he couldn't control the fate of the bird, he could at least control the story that would be told.

He shrugged his shoulders and said to the boys, "Just like the fate of the bird itself, the answer to your question is in your hands."

Then he turned back to his work and, as the boys stood there trying to figure out what to do next, Mr. Green looked over his shoulder and said, "I suggest you boys go over to your Grandma Lewis' house and ask her the same question."

Carlos had heard stories about Mr. Green from his grandma. "I bet those boys took the long way around Grandma Lewis' house on their way back to school," Carlos said with a little grin.

But then he got serious. He looked at Pete and said, "Sometimes I feel like I'm in the same situation as Mr. Green, only I don't have any good answers."

"Sometimes," Pete replied, "knowing there aren't any good answers is the best a person can do."

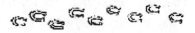

QUESTIONS: CHAPTER 5
Spring Break: A Leisurely Look at the Characteristics of Generational Poverty

The Woman in the Blue House on Oak Street

1. One son is responsible, works hard, and takes care of his mother. The other son is not responsible, plays, and uses his mother. Why do some adults only want to mess around and not be responsible for their lives?

2. One of the characteristics of generational poverty is that individuals live for relationships and entertainment. In the middle class, there is a strong emphasis on work and achievement. What would happen if everyone lived primarily for relationships and entertainment?

3. Why is the mother glad to see her son come back to her at the end? Would every mother be willing to welcome home a son who had stolen from her?

4. Which son is more like you? Why?

5. When one person takes all the time and another person gives all the time, each person resents the other. Why?

6. When the younger son returned, how would you have reacted if you were the mother? How would you have reacted if you were the older brother?

Little Eight John

1. Is it possible for someone to be born bad? Are you fated? In other words, can you do anything to change yourself, or are you destined to be the way you are? If you cannot make changes, then what is your life about? If you can make changes, why would you?

2. Do you believe you can make choices and changes?

3. Is it true that if you count your teeth a sickness will come upon your family? What are superstitions? Do they come true? What are some superstitions you have heard in your family or neighborhood?

4. When people make choices, and change who they are, do they lose friends?

5. Why is it hard to make changes in yourself? What are some things about you that you would like to change?

The Eagle Chick

1. "That old eagle lived and died a chicken, because that's what he thought he was." How do you know who you are?

2. Many people decide who they are based on what other people tell them. Who are you? Make a big T on a piece of paper. On the left-hand side make a list of 10 words that describe who you are. On the right-hand side, next to the word, tell what evidence you have that the descriptive word about you is true. Now tell what evidence you have that the word is not true.

3. People who soar above other people look at the sky. In other words, they have written goals and visions that they look at to help them decide who they are. Write down two personal goals for the next five years.

4. You are what you think you are. By changing your thoughts you can change who you are over time. Write down five statements about yourself. Each statement begins with: In five years I am _____ .

In Whose Hands Is the Fate of the Army

1. Does God help those who help themselves? What do you do each day that makes a difference in your life?

2. The Bible talks about free will. What does that mean?

3. How do you explain poverty? Wealth? Being educated? Being addicted? What part of a person's life can be changed? All? None?

4. How else could the General have made a decision? What might have happened if the General had not had a two-headed coin? How do you make decisions? What process do you use? What information do you gather before you make a decision?

5. Why do some people make decisions that get them into trouble?

6. Is it possible to make a decision by not making a decision?

The Story of Coach 'Stump' Barnes

1. In the story, Coach Barnes is quoted as saying, "If you want something badly enough, and are willing to work for it, you can accomplish lots more than a state championship." Is that true?

2. Sometimes things happen in an individual's life that changes the focus and direction of his or her life. Why can some individuals make the best of the situation and others cannot?

3. What is a difficulty that you have overcome? What did you do? How did you do it?

4. If you had been Pete, how would you feel?

Looking for Paradise

1. Is paradise a place or a state of mind? Is there anyplace that is perfect? Would you be in Paradise if you had a million dollars?

2. In order for plans to work, they have to be constantly questioned and adjusted. What could this man have done differently in order to reach Paradise?

3. Why is it that sometimes things work out for the best, even though they may not have been our plan?

4. Part of the man's trouble came from the fact he wouldn't say no: Why is the ability to say no important to success? What does saying no sometimes do to relationships?

5. Why might a man be happy in jail? But why doesn't jail solve his problems?

A Bird in the Hand

1. Why did the boys want to be smarter than Mr. Green?

2. Why were the boys willing to risk the life of a living thing just to make a point?

3. At the end of the story, Pete says, "Sometimes knowing there aren't any good answers is the best a person can do." Often in life, things are not clearly right or wrong. They are in between. How do you know what to do when there are no clear answers?

4. Some people make decisions based on the choice that does the least damage to the fewest people. Some people make decisions based on their own personal gain. Some people decide on the basis of what they want their friends to see. What factors do you consider when there are no clear answers?

CHAPTER 6

Role Models, Emotional Resources, and Decision-Making

"Where is he going?" Pete asked, nodding toward Carlos' friend Joey.

"He's headed home with a million ideas about his science project," Carlos answered.

"Are any of them good ideas?"

"Most of them. That is one thing about Joey: He usually has plenty of good ideas."

"Which one do you think he'll choose?" Pete wondered.

"He probably won't choose any," Carlos replied with a worried look on his face. "His grandma's been real sick, and his mother is busy with his baby brother. Plus, if any of the ideas cost money, he won't be able to do those. He'll probably come to school on

the day the project is due with a million excuses for not having it finished."

Pete watched Carlos think for a little while and then asked, "Do you have any ideas for your science project?"

"I might have one idea. Do you have any of those little jars that you planted your tomato seeds in this spring?"

"We can look." They got up to go around to the back of the house. "While we're looking, let me tell you a story."

A Million Ideas

A hunter dug a pit on the edge of the woods, hoping to trap an animal for his dinner. He carefully covered the pit with sticks and leaves and decided to come back later in the day to see if it was disturbed. Around mid-morning Fox was making his rounds in that part of the woods. He ran along the path, looking left and right, checking things out. He was wondering if Raccoon was sleeping. He was hoping Rabbit didn't hear him

182

coming. He was keeping one eye out for Field Mouse and looking up into the treetops imagining how pleasant it would be if Squirrel missed a jump and landed right in front of him on the path. Fox wasn't paying attention to where he was going, and he ran right into the hunter's trap.

Fox found himself at the bottom of the pit, looking up at the clear blue sky through a hole in the sticks and leaves. Do you think Fox was worried? Not a chance. Fox had a million ideas how to get out of that pit. In fact, to generate more ideas, he began to run around the bottom of the pit in circles, all the while thinking, "I have a million ideas! I have a million ideas! I have a million ideas for getting out of this trouble!" He ran and ran until a cloud of dust began to rise from the bottom of the pit.

A crane swooping above the pit flew into the cloud of dust and was blinded. She set herself down on the forest floor and became entangled in some sticks and leaves. Struggling to

183

free herself, she fell through the sticks and into the bottom of the hunter's trap. When her eyes grew accustomed to the light, she was dismayed and frightened to find herself at the bottom of a pit with Fox.

Fox took one look at Crane and began to laugh, "You stupid, frightened bird! Now you're in big trouble. The hunter will find you here and have you for dinner."

"Why are you so happy?" she asked. "You're in the same predicament."

"Yes," Fox replied, "but I have a million ideas how I can get out of this pit. But you? Look at you. You're too frightened to even think."

The crane did look scared and responded in a quavering voice, "I think I might have one idea."

"One idea!" the fox mocked. "Do you think you can get out of this pit with just one idea? I have a million ideas for getting out." Fox began to run in circles again, all the while chanting, "I have a million ideas. I have a million ideas. I have a million ideas for getting out of this pit!"

In the center of Fox's circle, Crane stood still. "I have one idea," she said. "I have one idea."

All afternoon Fox ran and chanted, "I have a million ideas! I have a million ideas!"

All afternoon Crane stood still in the middle of the pit. "I have one idea," she said.

As night began to fall, Fox ran faster and chanted louder, so he didn't hear the approach of the hunter. Even if he had heard the hunter coming—even if he had realized the sticks and leaves were being pulled away from the top of the pit—Fox would not have been afraid. He had a million ideas how he could get out of trouble.

The hunter looked down into his trap and smiled. "Aha!" he exclaimed. "Two for the price of one, and my friend, the fox, has already done half my work for me."

With that, Fox stopped running and looked at the still body of the crane lying in the center of the pit. "Foolish bird," he thought. "She has died of fright at the arrival of the hunter. Now she won't even be able to use her one idea. But I'm not afraid. I still have a million ideas!"

The hunter reached down into the bottom of the trap and hauled out the crane with one hand. He dropped the crane on the forest floor and reached for his gun to take care of the fox. In that moment, the hunter heard a great flapping of wings. Turning back, he saw the crane fly away over the treetops. That night, as the hunter ate fox stew and told his wife about the lovely fox-skin hat he planned to make for her, he shook his head in admiration at the single clever idea the crane used to escape his dinner pot.

"So, do you see anything you need for your project?" Pete asked.

Carlos held two jars up to the sunlight, turning them slowly in his hand. "I think these will do the trick."

"Go ahead and take 'em," Pete offered with a smile. "I won't be using them again."

Carlos plopped himself down on the step, un-zipped his backpack, and began messing with his books and papers. Pete watched with increasing curiosity and finally asked, "Are you looking for something in particular?"

"Nope," Carlos answered. "I'm just looking to make sure my math test didn't get lost when they were searching my backpack today."

"Who's 'they'? And what were 'they' searching for?" asked Pete, even more curious than before.

"At the start of math class, when Darnell was pulling his math book out of his backpack, a gun fell out onto the floor. Darnell tried to tell the teacher not to worry because the gun wasn't loaded, but she got all upset and called the office. Now Darnell probably can't come back to school, and everybody in the class had their backpacks searched. We never did get around to any math today. I wanted to make sure they didn't lose my test. I'm guessing the teacher will ask us to turn it in tomorrow. A lot of kids didn't have the test done. A few of them are probably hoping someone else brings a gun tomorrow."

"Why did he bring the gun to school in the first place?" Pete was shaking his head over this nonchalant conversation about guns he was having with a ten-year-old.

"Some big kids at the bus stop had been picking on him, and he wanted to show them he wasn't weak."

"When the gun fell on the classroom floor, it seems to me it was no longer a question of strength," Pete commented, "it was a question of intelligence."

Strength

Way back before there were buildings and lots of people here, when it was still mostly forest, some of the animals were bored one day and decided to have a contest to see who was the strongest. Buffalo, Bobcat, Deer, and Crawfish gathered in a clearing at the top of the big hill that overlooks the bay. They were ready to get started on the contest except for the fact that Man, who was fairly new to the area and had wanted a chance to compete, had not yet arrived. Before long they heard Man bustling through the woods. They always heard Man before he arrived. Just as the man got to the clearing, Buffalo saw him stop and lean over to put something in the thicket. Then Man came into the clearing and greeted the animals.

Buffalo, who had made himself in charge of the strength contest, explained the rules and told Crawfish to begin. Quick as could be, the crawfish slid to the center of the clearing and began to dig a huge mud chimney, which began to grow up and up until it reached Buffalo's snout. At that moment, Crawfish appeared at the top of the chimney and grabbed Buffalo by the nose with his big red claw. Buffalo snorted and shook his head but couldn't free himself of the little crustacean. Finally, Crawfish released the buffalo and dropped back onto his chimney. Raising both claws into the air, Crawfish proclaimed loudly, "STRENGTH!"

The other animals were amazed. "Wow," said Bobcat. "That's a pretty impressive display of strength!" Deer took a step back, not wanting to stick his nose into the conversation. Buffalo snorted, rubbed his snout in the mud, and nodded for Bobcat to show his strength.

With that, Bobcat growled and lunged forward, knocking down Crawfish's mud chimney with one swipe of his paw. Then he bared his claws and began to dig. Dirt flew in every direction.

The animals turned their heads away and covered their eyes. When the rain of earth ended, they turned back to the center of the clearing to find Bobcat missing—and a huge hole where he had been. They moved forward to look down into the hole. Bobcat let out a scream and sprung from the bottom of the hole up, right into the clearing, landing softly and deftly between Buffalo and Man. Bobcat licked the back of his paw, smiled, and purred loudly, "STRENGTH!"

"I guess so!" Crawfish agreed, unable to find even a remnant of the mud chimney he had built.

Buffalo grunted, "Remarkable display, Bobcat." Then he turned and nodded at Deer.

Deer shot out of the clearing and down the long hill, splashing her feet in the bay. Then she raced back up the long hill, all in less than thirty seconds. She stood once more where she had begun, the muscles in her flanks quivering. The animals were breathless with envy and respect at the power and strength Deer showed with each graceful leap.

"What a lovely display of strength," Buffalo commented. "Now it's my turn."

Buffalo turned and leaned his head against a tree. He pressed his full weight against the trunk and, with a splintering crash, the first tree gave way and knocked over the next and the next and the next. Buffalo raised his head and bellowed, shaking the splinters from his beard. He stood over the stack of trees he had broken and up-rooted. "That's STRENGTH!" he snorted.

Bobcat agreed wholeheartedly. Crawfish clicked his claws, "You are definitely the champ!"

"What about me? Do I get my chance?" The animals turned to Man.

"Well, sure. Of course. If you think that you are stronger than Buffalo, you get your chance," said Crawfish, speaking for the others.

Man backed up to the edge of the clearing and came running across the middle. He did two flips and a back somersault, landing in a puff of dust, hands above his head. "STRENGTH!" he shouted.

"That was impressive to look at," Buffalo replied, "and was certainly a grand display of flex-ibility and dexterity. But I wouldn't call it strength."

"Very nice," Deer added encouragingly,

"but I agree with Buffalo. I would hardly call that strength."

"You don't think so?" Man replied, anger in his voice. "Well, watch this!" With that Man raced across the clear-ing, quickly climbed to the top of a tree, grabbed a pine cone and flung it over the animals' heads. It struck a bunch of wild  grapes, which showered down on the animals be-neath. He scrambled back down the tree and stood before them, rubbing his hands together. "STRENGTH!" he proclaimed.

The animals finished eating the grapes and smacked their lips in appreciation. Buffalo re-sponded, "That was a nice gift, Man, and a ter-rific display of both agility and accuracy. But I wouldn't call that strength. Would any of you call that strength?" Buffalo asked looking at the other animals.

"It was fun to watch," Bobcat said, "but I wouldn't call it strength." Before any of the other animals could respond, Man shouted in anger.

"Oh, yeah?! You don't call that strength? Well, let's see what you call this."

Man ran to the edge of the clearing, where he had hidden something in the thicket. He reached in and pulled out a gun. Turning, he aimed the gun at the buffalo and pulled the trigger. KA-BLOOM!!!!

Buffalo fell to the ground with a thud, a cloud of dust billowing into the air. As the dust settled, Man thrust the gun above his head and shouted, "STRENGTH!"

He waited for the other animals to respond. Looking around, he saw that the animals had disappeared.

Later in the day, deep in the woods, Deer and Bobcat and Crawfish met and whispered together.

"What was that?" Deer asked.

"Was that strength?" Crawfish wondered.

"No," Bobcat replied. "That was not STRENGTH, that was DEATH."

With this understanding, the animals slid off into the woods and never came out to talk with Man again.

"Now when Man walks in the woods, he always walks alone. That's because Man is the only animal who isn't able to tell the difference between strength and death. Sounds to me like Man walks alone at the bus stop, too," Pete said. "You let me know if you ever have problems like Darnell. I could walk to school with you, and you could leave the gun at home."

Carlos looked up into the depth of Pete's eye. "Okay," he answered, "I'll let you know."

The next day after school, when Carlos stopped by the steps, he didn't take off his backpack, and he didn't take Pete up on his offer to get a cold orange soda out of the refrigerator.

"You got places to go?" Pete asked.

"I have to drop by and help Joey Robinson with his homework. You know, Joey's grandma died last week," Carlos offered as way of explanation.

"Was his grandma Mrs. Ford?" Pete asked. "I

think I might have seen Joey at the wake. Mrs. Ford was a pillar of this community."

"At school we all called her Cat Woman." Carlos didn't know much about her being a pillar, but he did know about her being an excuse.

Pete looked puzzled. "I don't recollect Mrs. Ford keeping any cats."

"Oh, we didn't call her Cat Woman because she kept cats. We called her Cat Woman because she died so many times. Every time Joey was absent from school, he always told the teacher it was because his grandma died. When he didn't have a project ready to hand in, or wasn't ready for a test, he said it was because his grandma died. One day the teacher mumbled something about Grandma Ford having nine lives. That's when we started calling her Cat Woman."

"There were folks in the neighborhood who thought she might just live forever," said Pete, "but she finally proved them wrong." He smiled at the thought of Grandma Ford and her tenacity. "So what's

Joey going to use for an excuse now?"

"We don't know," Carlos said, rising to his feet. "We think if he uses the one about his grandma again he might cry. So we all decided to help him with his homework until he can think up a new excuse. It might take a while. Joey's not one who thinks real well on his feet."

"I know the type," Pete grinned. "When I was growing up, there was a boy who lived off the county road with his mother. Another boy by the name of ... Joey."

Joey Brings Home His Pay

One day, when things were pretty bad financially, Joey's mother sent him down to the Grayson place because she heard there might be some work for him there.

"Work hard," she said. "At the end of the day, Mr. Grayson will give you a fair wage for your work. Make sure you bring your pay home to your mother."

Joey went whistling off to work. When he

got to the Grayson place, he was asked to hoe the garden. He worked all day under the hot sun and, when day was done, he was given one shiny silver dime for his toils. On the way home, just past Judge

Watson's place, Joey was admiring that coin, flipping it into the air and watching as the rays of the setting sun glinted from its shiny surface. But as he crossed over a creek, he dropped the coin and sadly watched it roll off the edge of the bridge into the water.

When he got home, his mother asked him how much he got paid. Her face lit up when he told her about the dime. Of course, she wanted Joey to show her the dime. "To see the dime you will have to jump into the creek," Joey said. Then he told her how he had lost his wages.

"You foolish child," Joey's mother scolded. "You should have put your wages in your pocket."

"Tomorrow I will," Joey promised.

The next day Joey went whistling off to work. When he got to the Grayson place he was put to weeding the tomato patch. He worked all day under the hot sun and, when day was done, he was given a large jar of milk for his wages. Joey poured that jar of milk into his pocket as his mother told him. By the time he passed Judge Watson's place, his pants were all sticky and stinky.

When Joey's mother held out her hand and asked for his wages, he opened his pocket and showed her the mess he had made.

"You foolish child," Joey's mother scolded. "You should have carried that jar of milk on top of your head where no harm would have come to it."

"Tomorrow I will," Joey promised.

The next day Joey went whistling off to work. When he got to the Grayson place, he was put to work picking strawberries. The sun beat down on Joey's back as he bent over the strawberry plants, filling up baskets with sweet red berries. He worked all day under the hot sun and, when day was done, he was given a block of butter for his wages. Remembering his mother's advice, he took off his hat, put the butter on his head, replaced the hat, and started walking home. By the time he passed Judge Watson's place, the butter was nearly all melted and had dripped down around his ears, sliding down his spine and into his pants.

Joey's mother took one look and guessed what had happened. "You silly son," she said. "You should have wrapped your wages in cold leaves from the spring and held it tight in your hands."

"Tomorrow I will," Joey promised.

The next day Joey went whistling off to work. Mr. Grayson sent Joey to shovel out the cow stalls. The barn was hot, and the stench was horrible, but Joey worked hard shoveling and hauling manure out into the field behind the barn. All day he toiled under the hot sun and, when day was done, Mr. Grayson let Joey choose the pick of the litter of puppies that the sheep dog was raising in the corner of the barn. Joey, re-membering his mother's advice, stopped and wrapped that puppy in cold leaves from the spring. Then he held the puppy tight in his hands. By the time he passed Judge Watson's place, the puppy was shivering and squirming. Joey held that puppy even tighter. When he got it home, it was nearly dead and certainly not much good for anything.

"You thick child," his mother said. "You don't have the brains God gave a goose! Next time, tie a string around it and pull it along behind you."

"Tomorrow I will," Joey promised.

The next day, Joey went whistling off to work. Mr. Grayson set him to work mending the fence railings. Joey lifted and pulled and pounded. All day he toiled under the hot sun and, when day was done, Mr. Grayson gave Joey a big old ham for his pay. Joey immediately pulled some string out of his pocket, tied it around the ham and dragged that piece of meat home behind him. By the time he got to Judge Watson's place, the ham was pretty well shredded and embedded with gravel and dirt.

His mother took one look and said, "Hello! The lights are on, but no one is home! Next time carry it up on your shoulder."

"Tomorrow I will," Joey promised.

The next day Joey went whistling off to

work. Mr. Grayson handed Joey a paintbrush and a bucket of paint and put him to work sprucing up the chicken coop. All day he toiled under the hot sun and, when day was done, Mr. Grayson gave Joey a donkey.

Now Joey was a strapping young man, but it was some time before he managed to wrestle that donkey up onto his shoulders. When he had accomplished the feat, he started staggering home under the weight of his wages. It just so happened, as he carried that donkey past Judge Watson's house, the judge's daughter was gazing out the window of her second-floor bedroom. The judge's daughter was a pretty young thing, but sickly and depressed since her mother had died. The doctor had informed the judge that his daughter didn't need medicine, but could benefit greatly from laughter. When she saw Joey stumbling down the road with a donkey wrapped around his shoulders, she got just what the doctor ordered. She laughed so hard she nearly burst. The judge came out of the house and offered Joey a job the following day keeping his daughter company.

As luck would have it, Joey was good company, the daughter got on the road to recovery, and the judge paid Joey's wages directly to Joey's mother.

Carlos smiled as he got up to go help his friend Joey with his math.

"Make sure Joey stands up while he does that math homework," Pete said. "Sounds to me like that boy needs to learn to think on his feet. In the meantime, tell him I have a few lives left in me. If he doesn't get his homework finished, he can always come to my funeral."

Carlos was sipping on an orange soda, watching as the Reverend Johnson came out of his house, walked by his car, and headed up the street to the bus station. Between swigs of soda, he looked over at Pete. "Why is Reverend Johnson taking the bus when he has a car right there in the street?"

"That old car hasn't been running since winter," Pete answered.

"My teacher took the bus to school today. I saw her getting off on my way to school, so I helped her carry her stuff. She carries a whole lot of stuff. She said her car was sick, too."

Pete smiled. "I think the Reverend's car may not be sick," he said. "I think the Reverend's car may be dead."

"I believe you got that right. One thing for sure, I don't want to be a Reverend or a teacher when I grow up. They can't even afford to keep their wheels running."

"So, what are you planning to be when you grow up?" Pete asked.

"Depends on how much I grow," Carlos said, looking at his puny little hands. "If I can't be an NBA star, I'm not sure what's left."

Pete looked at his small friend slugging down the orange soda, wondering what might become of him. "Well, keep your eyes open ... you might see someone doing something you want to do when you grow up. It's a hard choice, but you'll probably find *something you're really good at."*

"Like what?" Carlos asked.

"You never know."

The Best Thief

I had a friend once who had two older brothers. All three of those boys had favorite uncles that looked after them from time to time. The oldest brother's favorite uncle was a boot maker, and the boy hung around him long enough to become pretty good at making boots. The next brother's favorite worked on cars, and that boy hung around him long enough to become pretty good at fixing cars. Now the youngest boy's favorite uncle was a thief, and he watched him work for a long time before the boy thought he was ready to go into official training.

"You think you'd like to become a thief?" his uncle asked. "Let me see if you're ready to accept the challenge. See that chicken's nest?" he asked, pointing into the neighbor's backyard. "I'm going to sneak over there and steal the eggs out of that nest without the chicken ever being the wiser. Then we'll see if you can sneak them back into the nest before the chicken realizes they're gone."

The thief sneaked into the yard and without him even knowing, my friend sneaked right behind. The uncle slipped an egg out from under that chicken and put it into his coat pocket. My friend slipped the egg out of his uncle's pocket 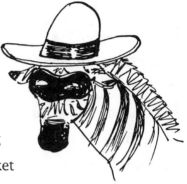 and put it into his own. Then the uncle took two more eggs and put them into his pocket. Each time, the boy slipped them out and put them into his own pocket. He crept back over to his uncle's place without the uncle ever knowing.

"That hen never even let out a cluck," his uncle said, reaching into his pocket for the eggs. "Take these eggs ... " He patted his coat pocket, then checked the other pocket, searching for the eggs.

"You mean these eggs?" the boy asked.

Over a breakfast of eggs and toast, the uncle decided the boy was ready to learn to be a thief. They studied and worked for about six months. Finally, the uncle decided the boy might be ready to work on his own.

"I can't turn you loose until I'm sure," he said. "Otherwise, you'll mess things up and make it hard on me. I'm going to give you three jobs. If you manage to complete them successfully, I'll retire and let you be the best thief in the county. Here's the first test. Down at the end of the county road, there's a junkyard. Tonight I want you to go down there and, while the junkman and his wife are sleeping, I want you to take the sheets out from under them without them being the wiser. To make it a challenge, I'll let them know you're coming."

My friend planned all day. At midnight he snuck into the funeral parlor and stole a corpse from a casket due to be buried in the morning. He put some bricks in the empty casket and closed it. Then he hauled the corpse down to the junkyard and started pushing it up against the junkman's bedroom window. The third time he raised that corpse up to the window, two shots rang out. My friend threw the body down and hid behind an old car.

The boy heard the junkman's wife scream, "You get that body off our property! If you don't, the police will be down here tomorrow asking questions that you may not want to answer."

The junkman came out of the house, hoisted the body up over his shoulder, and headed out into the fields with a shovel in his hand. My friend waited for a little while, then he went into the house and right into the bedroom. He plopped into the junkman's bed and groaned, "Whew! That body sure was heavy!" Quietly, he slipped the sheets off his side of the bed.

Then he rolled over and said to the junkman's wife, "I'm hot and sticky from burying that body. You need to let me sleep by the window." So the wife got up and stumbled over to the other side of the bed, too tired to realize the sheets were gone. The thief waited until he heard the woman's quiet breathing, then he wrapped himself up in the rest of those sheets and crept out of the house and back to his uncle's.

His uncle congratulated him on passing the first test, but he warned that the second test would be even harder. "Do you know that dirt farmer who works the rocky ground out on the Williams place?"

The young man guessed he knew him. Everybody for miles knew him. He was the meanest man in the county. Made mean, people said, from watching his family starve while he tried to scratch out a living on the worst property for miles.

"Tomorrow he's going to try again to plow that land. While he's plowing, I want you to steal his plow mule. It's an easy enough task for a young man striving to be the best thief in the county, so I warned him you were coming, and he'll be watching out for you."

All night long my friend lay awake wondering how he would steal that mule. The next morning, on his way out to the Williams place, he searched the fence rows until he found what he was looking for. He reached down into the tall grass and plucked a mother rabbit and three little bunnies out of a nest. He stuck the rabbits into a tote bag. When he got to the fields, he saw the man out trying to plow his land. The farmer had a gun poking out of his pants, and he was cursing the day he got stuck working in those rocky fields.

As the farmer turned the mule around and headed toward his end of the field, the thief, hiding in the fence row, let loose of one of the baby rabbits. As it scampered across the field, the man pulled his gun out and shot at it. On each pass of the plow, the thief let loose another bunny and listened for the gunshots. Finally, the thief released the mother rabbit. She was big enough to make a pot of rabbit stew that could feed a family. The farmer dropped the reins, grabbed his gun, and started chasing after the mother rabbit. You could hear the shots ringing out as he followed that rabbit across field after field until he was out of sight. Then the young man unhitched the mule and led it back to his uncle.

His uncle congratulated him on his success and explained that the third task would be a little harder. "Tomorrow I'm going to go out to the big ranch north of town and steal a sheep. Your task will be to steal the sheep from me before I get back to town. But be careful, I may be carrying my gun, too."

Early the next morning the young man stopped by his oldest brother's boot shop to borrow the best looking boots in the store. Then he went to his other brother and asked for a ride out to the river road on the way to the ranch north of town. There he waited for his uncle to walk by on his way to the ranch.

After his uncle had passed, he took one of those beautiful boots and set it in the middle of the road. He took the other boot and walked some distance back toward town, across the river bridge and around a bend. Then he put the other boot in the middle of the road and hid in the trees.

Pretty soon the uncle came walking down the road leading a stolen sheep. He had his eye out for anything out of the ordinary. He saw the

boot in the road long before he got to it. When he did get to it, he noticed it wasn't just any old boot. He picked it up and admired the workmanship.

"What a shame. It's a beautiful boot, and my size too. But what good is one without the match? It's only a burden to all but a one-legged man." He threw it back down and led the sheep back toward town. Before long he crossed the river bridge and rounded the curve, only to see, sitting right there in the middle of the road, the mate to that lost boot.

"What a fool! I should have picked up the other one." He quickly tied his sheep to a bush and ran back to get the other boot. When he came back and found his sheep gone, he knew he had been tricked. Not to be outdone, the uncle went back to the ranch and stole a second sheep. Leading this new sheep back to town, he crossed the river bridge and rounded the curve. At the spot where he had found the second boot, he heard the bleating of a sheep coming from the trees by the river.

"I overestimated the cleverness of my young nephew," he thought to himself. "My sheep wasn't stolen, it only came loose and wandered off." So, like the boots, thinking two were better than one, the uncle tied up the second sheep and went off searching for the first. The bleating took him farther and farther from the road. Finally, he gave up the search and headed back to the second sheep tied by the road. Of course, it was gone when he got there, for the young man had led his uncle on the wild-goose chase, bleating like a sheep until he could double back and steal the second sheep.

When the uncle got back to his house, the young man already had the sheep butchered and in the barbecue pit. Later, over a leg of mutton, the uncle proclaimed my friend the best thief in the county.

Carlos licked his lips, imagining the taste of that barbecue sauce. "What happened to your friend when he grew up?"

Pete smiled and winked at Carlos. "He took all that training and put it to good use; he became sheriff of the county. Eventually, he went into politics and was elected county judge. As judge, he figured he could make sure no one ever took over his claim to being best thief in the county.

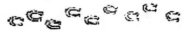

"See you tomorrow," Joey said to Carlos as they approached Pete's house. "Man, am I glad tomorrow is Saturday. I'll be coming over in the morning. I have to get home now, or my mama will be mad at me." As Joey walked away, Carlos waved then dropped his backpack on the step. Joey rounded the corner, heading home, still chattering to himself.

"I believe that boy must talk all night in his sleep," Pete said, grinning.

"That's why I'm late," said Carlos. "Joey had detention again. I was waiting for him because it's my day to make sure he brings his books home."

"Is he doing okay since his grandma died?"

Carlos thought for a minute, then answered: "He's doing all right, but he chooses the worst times to do dumb stuff. Before you know it he's in trouble and he doesn't even know what he's done."

"If he keeps messing up," Pete noted, "sooner or later he'll learn to make the right choice at the right time. I once heard a story about a kid just like Joey."

The Gardener's Son's Quest

The governor and his lovely daughter were living in the governor's mansion when the governor became ill. All the doctors looked for a cure, but the only thing they found to help the illness were the apples that grew on the tree outside the governor's window. You can imagine the governor kept a close watch on that tree, even counting the number of apples from the time  they were the size of an eyeball. One year, just as the apples were getting ripe, the governor was awakened in the night by the cry of a bird. When he reached the window, he saw a large bird in the branches of his apple tree. The bird's feathers seemed to collect the light of the moon and reflect it throughout the garden. When the bird saw movement at the governor's window, it snatched an apple from the tree and flew up over the garden wall.

"The gardener is going to hear from me in the morning," the governor mumbled. "It's his job to protect my apples!"

The governor pulled a chair up to the window and did not sleep for the rest of the night. By sunrise, he was tired and cranky and not sure he could believe his gardener's promise.

"You will not lose another apple," the gardener assured him. "I have three sons, and all are expert marksmen. I will put one on the night watch."

When night came, the oldest of the boys leaned a chair against the garden wall and waited, a rifle in his lap. At midnight, the governor was wide awake and heard the flapping of wings. He rushed to the window and saw the bird once again in his tree. The son on guard was sound asleep in his chair. "Wake up, you idiot! There's that bird again."

The boy awoke with a start and fumbled with his gun. The bird snatched the finest apple on the tree. Bird and apple were gone before the boy could get off a shot.

After a day of hearing the governor's fuming and threats, the gardener sent his second son to guard the tree, warning him to stay awake and do his job. At midnight, however, the bird was back, the boy was asleep, and the governor's shouts rang out. The boy awoke in time to get off an errant shot, but not soon enough to save the apple.

The gardener promised better results from his youngest son, and the governor held out some hope, for he had heard the boy was clever and bright, though a bit like your friend Joey and prone to be impulsive at inappropriate moments. That night at midnight the governor was awake and chatting with the boy from his window when they heard the flapping of wings. The bright light reflecting off the bird's feathers lit the garden like daylight. The bird no sooner landed in the branches of the tree than a shot rang out. The bullet struck the bird on its wing. It faltered for a moment, and then as a single feather floated to the ground, the bird rose with a screech and flew over the garden wall. The governor came into the garden to congratulate the boy. On close inspection, they found that the feather was heavier than lead. It turned out to be pure gold.

The next day the boy's picture was on the

front page of the paper and, for a week, he re-mained on night watch. The bird was not to be seen again. Throughout the week the governor stood watch by his window studying the golden feather he held constantly in his hand. By the end of the week he announced he would give his daughter and his summerhouse on the beach to anyone who could bring him, dead or alive, the bird with the golden feathers.

The gardener's oldest son was the first to set off in search of the bird, because that's the way these stories go. Of course, he didn't have much success, though he certainly had the op-portunity. In the middle of the afternoon he sat down to eat a sandwich that he had packed for his journey. He had taken the first bite when a scroungy hound dog walked out of the woods and sat down in front of him, tilting its head to one side as it eyed the boy's lunch. Then the dog spoke (because this is one of those stories with talking animals), asking for half of the boy's sandwich.

"Or maybe you could spare a few of those potato chips," the dog begged.

But the boy took up a rock and chunked it at the mutt. Even though the stone bounced off his ribs like a drop of water, the dog backed up a safe distance and shouted to the boy, "Bad style, son. But since I've heard you have a younger brother who is a bit smarter and perhaps a bit kinder, I will give you a piece of advice. By sunset you will come to a village. On one side of the street you will see a hotel and club with loud music and young men and women dancing, drinking, and having a good time. On the other side of the street is an old, run-down house with a single light. My fleas tell me you should take lodging from the husband and wife who live there with their little child."

Given the choice, the boy headed straight for the loud music, and there we will leave him.

A week later the second son set out, and you can imagine where he ended up. He met the same dog, got the same advice, and ended up at the same party with his brother. When a week passed, the youngest son set out, and I'm sure it's no surprise to you that he sat under the same tree and was willing to share his lunch with that raggedy old hound dog. The dog wasn't disappointed. Before offering his assistance in the boy's quest for the golden bird, he told him about the

town up ahead and waited to see if he would follow good advice or party with his brothers.

The clever boy avoided the loud music and
laughter and was welcomed into the couple's little
house where he was fed and had a good night's
sleep. The next morning he was up and on his
way before the early news. He was not a mile out
of town when he saw his canine friend sitting at
the side of the road, scratching with his hind paw
the fleas behind his ears.

"Good morning, friend," said the boy.

"And the same to you," replied the dog.
"Have you any idea how far you have to travel to
find the bird with the golden feathers?"

"I haven't a clue," the boy replied.

"Well, I happen to have heard that a big
football star has the bird in his mansion just north
of the city."

"It will take three or four days to get there,"
the boy calculated.

"Not if you take the greyhound," the dog
replied. "Hop on my back, and I'll make the trip
short."

The boy looked at the bony hound and
debated. But when the dog threatened to leave

219

him behind, the boy climbed onto the dog's back, and away they flew, faster than a moment's thought. They overtook the wind that was before them, and the wind that came after did not overtake them. By mid-afternoon they stopped to rest outside the stucco wall of the mansion, and there they waited until the sun had set.

"Here's the plan," the dog said. "I'll go ahead, disarm the security system, and take care of the guard dogs. You come after and enter the front hall. Go from room to room until you find the golden bird. If you have your share of good sense, you will slip the bird and cage straight out the door, and no one will be the wiser. If you haven't got your share, then I can't help you and no one else can either."

Ten minutes later the boy climbed the fence and walked, big as you please, right through the front door. In the first room a dozen Dobermans dozed in front of a lighted trophy cabinet. In the next, half a dozen pit bulls snoozed around a glass case that held a Super Bowl ring. In the next room three German shepherds snored beneath a framed photo of the football star with the President. The next room had neither guard nor light, but it shone brightly, for there on a table perched the golden bird in a common wood-and-wire cage. On the table next to the cage were the governor's apples, turned to solid gold, beside a beautiful golden cage.

The boy thought it would be a pity to leave the golden cage behind, for it was much better suited to the bird than the common cage he was in. Maybe, he thought, with all the trophies, it wouldn't be missed. Maybe, he thought, he could just slip out with it, and no one would catch him. But my guess is that, like your friend Joey, he didn't think at all. He opened up the golden cage and tried to put the bird inside. As soon as the bird's wing brushed the bars of that cage, the bird let out a squawk that would raise the dead! Before the boy had another thought, he was surrounded by snarling guard dogs and the football star himself.

"I should call the police right now," the football player said, "but I don't need the publicity. Besides, if you are brave enough to come in here, maybe we can make a deal. In the next city to the north there's an agent who has more money and a bigger house than I have. He also has a racehorse that can outrun the wind. If you can bring that horse to me, I'll give you the golden bird and forget I ever saw you here tonight."

Not sure where to turn next, the boy left, feeling more than a little stupid for failing to follow the dog's directions. As luck would have it, the dog was waiting for him.

"Hop on. We'll go and see if you have learned a thing today."

The boy climbed onto the dog's back, and off they went, faster than a moment's thought. They overtook the wind that was before them, and the wind that came after did not overtake them. The boy and dog were soon outside another mansion. This one was bigger than the first with, not only a wall and a security system, but also an armed guard and a moat. Within the wall, the boy spied the roof of the stables. They waited until night came.

"Here's the plan," the dog said. "I'll go ahead, disarm the security system, and take care of the guards. You come after, take the filly by the reins, and lead her out. But be careful not to let her touch the gates, or the fences, or anything except her hooves to the ground. If you have your share of good sense, you'll be riding that horse within the hour. If you haven't your share, you'll be in worse shape than you were before."

Off went the dog and, fifteen minutes later, the boy followed. When he approached the

stables, he saw two rows of armed guards, each in a deep sleep. Right through the middle of them the boy marched, directly into the stable. There he found a stable boy with a curry comb, and another with a bridle, and a third and fourth with a bag of oats and a handful of hay. Each was as stiff and gray as a statue. The filly was the only thing that showed a spark of life. She was a beautiful horse, standing tall with a common wood-

and-leather saddle on her back. But a fine-tooled saddle made of solid gold hung nearby. The boy thought it a shame to leave without it.

I don't have to tell you what happened next. The filly bumped into something while the boy tried to switch saddles. The next thing you know, he was surrounded by armed men with walkie-talkies. The agent was called to the scene, and the only thing that kept the boy off the front pages was the agent's penchant for closing a deal.

Moments later the boy was outside the mansion walls wondering how he was going to get to an oil baron's ranch. He had been told he would never see the filly or the golden bird unless he could kidnap the oil baron's beautiful daughter and bring her back to the agent. Lucky for him, he just happened to run into his friend, the dog. The dog just happened to know the way to the oil baron's ranch.

"Were you behind the door when God was passing out brains?" the dog asked. "Get on my back. We have a long trip ahead of us." Off they went, faster than a moment's thought. They overtook the wind that was before them, and the wind that came after did not overtake them. By nightfall the boy and dog were eating their sandwiches near a mansion as big as the last two put together.

"Here's the plan," the dog said, and he promised to make things right just as before. "But be careful," he warned. "Don't let the girl touch a doorway or wall with so much as a thread of clothes or a single hair from her head. And don't stop to do anyone a favor. If you do, I'm afraid I can't help you." With that, the dog went ahead and, shortly thereafter, the boy followed.

Now you would have thought when the boy entered the mansion and saw all those sleeping guards and dogs, he would have had the good sense to follow the dog's directions. But when he got to the room where the oil baron and his daughter were sleeping, he took one look at that girl and fell in love. He stared at her for the longest time and finally bent over and kissed her. She opened her eyes and would have shouted out in anger or fear, except the boy was a handsome hunk, and he had that silly love-grin on his face. It took that boy five or six whispering starts before he could explain why he was there and what he needed her to do. After he assured her that he would come up with a scheme so she wouldn't have to spend the rest of her life, or even a minute, with that sleazy agent, she agreed to go with him. But before she left, she asked permission to kiss her father goodbye.

"No way!" the boy said. "No favors allowed."

She gave him such a pitiful look, then a second look he couldn't describe but wanted to see about a thousand more times. So he said she could give her father a little kiss. "But be careful not to wake him."

As soon as her lips touched his forehead, he awoke, along with all the dogs and guards.

"Geez!" the boy said, slapping himself in the head with the palm of his hand. "Why does this happen to me?" Within minutes he was given a pickax and assigned to chip away at a giant boulder that was blocking the flow of the baron's oil, as well as the morning sunlight into the east windows of the house. The problem was that for each chip off the boulder, two more "grew" on. The boulder got bigger as the day went along. It was pretty discouraging knowing the only way to leave with the girl was to break down that stone. The one thing that kept him from giving up was the look the girl gave him when she brought out fresh lemonade. At the rate he was going, he realized he might see that look a million times before he broke down the boulder. At the end of the day he headed for the mansion. On the way he spied his friend, the dog, gave him the leftovers from his lunch, and scratched him behind the ears.

"Don't worry," the dog said. "I'll think of something."

The next morning the boy awoke with the sun shining through his bedroom window and the sound of oil gushing out of the ground. The dog sat near the oil well, looking up at the boy with a goofy canine grin on his face. The boy understood that the movement of boulders is no great task for a dog with the power to fly.

By noon they had finished celebrating and saying their goodbyes and were off on that dog's back quick as a moment's thought. They overtook the wind that was before them, and the wind that came after did not overtake them. By the time school was out they were at the rich agent's house. The boy and the girl went into the stable, and the trade was made for the horse. When the boy jumped up on the horse's back, he asked if he might shake hands with the girl and wish her well.

"Why, certainly," said the agent, who always felt smug after he negotiated a sneaky deal. In his smugness he didn't notice the handshake linger until the boy had the baron's daughter sitting snugly behind him on the golden saddle. Off they raced to the football star's house. The boy entered alone, holding the horse's reins.

Out came the golden birdcage, apples, and all. The boy could not take leave of the horse without rubbing its nose. As he stroked its flank, he leapt onto the horse's back, the golden items in hand, and raced toward home. He stopped only to pick up the oil baron's daughter.

Now I know your mama is calling, so pay close attention, because I'm going to spin this story out in a hurry. The governor's daughter was glad to see the gardener's son, but none too happy about the oil baron's daughter. That night, as the two girls gave each other the evil eye, the dog came to the rescue again. He got up and stretched, and then, to everyone's amazement, he leapt into the fire! Fur and fleas were burnt up, and from the fire emerged a handsome young man who claimed to be free at last of a wicked spell, broken when he helped the gardener's son succeed on his quest. I know that's hard to believe, but you can do it. You believed in a talking dog all the way through the story.

At any rate, the handsome new man got a job on the governor's staff and eventually hooked up with the governor's daughter. The oil baron's daughter stayed sweet on the gardener's son, and that's that.

Carlos sat for a minute taking it all in. He jumped up to go when he heard his mama call him. "And did the gardener's son learn not to make stupid choices?"

"Nope," Pete said. "But now he's rich, and his dumb choices don't surprise folks anymore. Now hurry home, before your mama gets mad at _me_!"

QUESTIONS: CHAPTER 6
Role Models, Emotional Resources, and Decision-Making

A Million Ideas

1. The fox had a million ideas. The crane had one. Yet the crane escaped alive. The crane acted upon an idea, while the fox merely talked about his ideas. Why was the crane successful in surviving?

2. A strategy is a way to deal with a situation. Why is having a strategy you can use important for survival? Where do you learn these strategies? An idea is what to do; a strategy is how to do it. What strategy do you use to make a friend? What strategy do you use to work for a boss or teacher you don't like?

3. The fox was so busy thinking inside his head he didn't pay attention to what was happening outside his head. He didn't hear the hunter. He believed the crane was dead. Have you ever missed important details in your surroundings? What can you do to be alert (at the same time) to what is inside your head and what is outside your head?

Strength

1. At the end of the story the bobcat says, "That was not STRENGTH, that was DEATH." What is the difference?

2. Which takes more strength—killing, or working to be better or stronger?

3. Why did the man kill? When is killing about self-defense? When is killing about winning? When is killing about proving a point?

4. Why is the display of strength or intelligence or ability or agility or cunning or coping always related to a specific task? Can a person show those traits in one situation and not in another? Has there been a time in your life when you were strong in one situation but not strong in another? Why? Is there anything you can do about that?

5. How else could the man have handled the situation other than killing? Would it have been okay for the man to admit he wasn't the strongest? What would it have cost the man to admit that? Would he himself have been killed?

Joey Brings Home His Pay

1. One coping strategy that is very helpful to survival is the ability to "think on your feet." What does that mean?

2. Joey has no common sense. What does common sense mean?

3. Joey does whatever he's told to do regardless of the situation. How does that help Joey? How does that hurt Joey?

4. Over time a "tool box" of strategies can be developed so that a person can use the right strategy for the right situ-

ation. Have you ever tried to solve a problem with a strategy that worked in the past? Have you ever failed to solve a problem with a strategy that worked in the past?

5. What would you do if you were Joey's mother?

6. In the end Joey is successful because the situation is tailor-made for him. His job is to entertain, and his pay is given directly to his mother. His situation works with his personal strengths. What are your personal strengths? In other words, what do you do well?

7. One way to cope and survive is to find situations that work with your personal strengths. What situations would do that for you?

The Best Thief

1. A role model or mentor is someone you learn from, someone who teaches you the "what" and "how" of a job or task. The uncle is a role model for the young man. Why does the young man want to be better at the job than the uncle?

2. A role model often provides emotional resources. In other words, he or she teaches a person how to handle a situation emotionally. Who is a role model for you? What have you learned from that person? Sometimes a role model teaches you how NOT to do something. Have you had such a role model? What have you learned not to do?

3. A role model may give a strategy or way to handle an angry customer or your own angry feelings. Role models

often use a technique called "reframing." Reframing is when you help a person see a situation another way. Can you give an example of a way a role model has helped you see a situation another way?

4. Pete says the boy "took all that training and put it to good use; he became sheriff of the county." Why did the boy choose to use his training for something that was legal rather than illegal? Why is working for the good of people and society more rewarding than working against people and society?

5. Why didn't the boy say to himself, "I will be the best thief ever. Society has never done nothin' for me. I'll teach them"? How did the boy reframe the situation so that his skills were beneficial for everyone? What skill(s) do you have that you could use to make the world a better place?

6. Margaret Wheatley, in her video "Leadership and the New Science," relates that scientists are finding that a butterfly's wings flapping in Japan can change the weather patterns in other parts of the world. What is one little thing you could do tomorrow that would make a positive difference for someone you know? Would it hurt you in any way to do that kindness for another person?

The Gardener's Son's Quest

1. Some people seem to come out of bad situations "smelling like a rose" (in other words, they are successful in spite of themselves). Why does this happen?

2. Sometimes there are individuals in a person's life who

give good advice, but the person ignores it. Why is the good advice ignored? Is there someone in your life who gives you good advice that you ignore? Is there someone you give good advice to but he or she ignores it? Why does this happen?

3. A support system is a group of people on whom you rely for help and assistance. Who is your support system?

4. How can a support system help someone? Can it hurt them? If so, how?

5. When a person shifts from one culture to another, from poverty to middle class or from middle class to wealth or from being uneducated to educated, there is a period of time when that person feels alone. He or she doesn't feel comfortable with the friends they had before because they don't have much in common. Yet they don't feel comfortable with the friends in the group they are moving into because they don't have much in common yet with them either. During this time of being alone, it's very easy to get involved with habits (alcohol, drugs, people, etc.) that are harmful. What can a person do during these times of aloneness to keep on keeping on?

CHAPTER 7

Support Systems: Use and Abuse

"You look worried. Is something wrong with your mama?" Pete knew Carlos wanted to talk or he wouldn't have been hanging around.

"No, Mama is doing all right. Just some aching in her bones."

"Well, if it's not your mama, what's the deal?"

"Ever since Joey's grandmother died, he hasn't been the same. He quit joking. He even quit talking. I can't get him to smile. I can't even make him mad. I think I might as well give up."

"He's too good a friend to give up on. You at least need to try everything you know."

"That's the problem. I just don't know anything else to do."

"I knew some kids once who got into a tough

situation and weren't sure what to do," Pete recalled,
sitting down next to Carlos on the step.

The Seven Sisters' Situation

When I was growing up, I knew a man who had seven daughters. That was a house full of women, I'll tell you. It didn't surprise one person in town when that man volunteered to go fight in Korea. He claimed he was going to get his pay-

check doing his patriotic duty, but we all guessed that his house had too many women for just one man. That man wasn't gone six months when those girls' mama took sick and died. They were afraid to tell anyone because they didn't want to be sent off, with their daddy not knowing where they were. So they had a secret meeting and made a pact. Each would do the best of what they could do, and together they would see if they could make it.

The first sister said she was good at waiting, and she would be patient and wait out those troubled times until the war was over and her daddy came home. She set the tone for those other girls. She was stoic about waiting. When the girls got scared at night, she said, "You just watch, I'm going to wait until the sun comes up before I get scared." When the sun came up, and the girls looked at their problems in the light of day, it didn't seem like there was that much to be scared about. That sister waited for the postman every day to bring letters from her daddy. She waited every evening to be the last one served. On many evenings, she went without and had to wait until the next day to eat.

The second sister was full of assurance. She let those girls know every day they were going to make it. "We are doing just fine," she said. "We can do this. We can make it until our daddy comes home. When our daddy comes home, he's going to walk down that road and see each of his girls, strong and healthy and happy to see him." That girl could talk the bad right out of any situation. Why, she could make the sun shine on the dark side of the street just by crossing over.

They called the third sister "first-then." She could talk as well as the second sister, but she always talked "in a line." Before the girls went to bed each night, she would tell them how tomorrow had to go. "First we have to be up before the sun rises, then we can get our chores finished before school. First we have to get dressed, then fetch the water, make the grits, and clean the dishes. Next we have to ... " She could see the whole day in her head and walk her sisters through it step by step.

The one in the middle was the one who talked to God. She listened to her sisters, but she said, "I get my guidance from the Lord." Every night she read out loud from the Bible. The last words on her lips at night were words of prayer, and the first words in the morning were words of thanks to the Lord for each new day. On Sunday mornings, when some of those sisters wanted to sleep, she said, "There is no rest for the weary. We have to go to church." I believe that God looked kindly on those girls and answered a good share of that sister's prayers.

The fifth sister was the most outgoing of the all those girls. She was friendly and funny and the sort of person who was good to be around. She made many friends, and many days it was the advice of those friends that helped the girls survive. It was her friends who told them to put newspaper over the windows during the cold spells so that their house would stay warm. It was her friends who told them how to fill out the papers to get assistance. It was her friends who told her where to pick wild greens and onions to cook in soup.

The sixth sister didn't have many friends because she was not as talkative; she was much more serious than her sisters. But she did strike up a relationship with a widow woman who lived in a tumble-down, peely paint, wood-frame shack down by the creek past the railroad track. Lots of folks in town talked about that woman and were afraid of her. Some said she was an Indian woman, and I believe she might have been part Indian. Some said she was a witch, and I remember none of the children in town ever went around her house at Halloween. But this sister didn't seem scared of her at all. Even though the sixth sister sometimes went without eating, she often took food to that old woman. Some believed that the old woman had her under a spell, but I think the sister went to her because she realized the old woman had to know a whole lot in order to survive by herself for so many years. Some of the things she learned from the old woman she shared with her sisters.

The youngest sister in the family wasn't just quiet, she was nearly silent. She was so little when her daddy left and her mama died that she didn't even remember having parents. She watched how the other kids went home to their parents every day. She watched how those families played and how they worked. She watched how they suffered and how they survived. She watched where they planted their vegetables and when they picked their melons. She watched and watched and, very quietly, she showed her sisters the things that she learned.

In the end, it was the oldest sister who was waiting and the youngest sister who was watching, who first saw their daddy coming down the road with a seaman's bag over his shoulder. After he said a proper goodbye to their mama and built a cross for her grave, he told those girls that they were finished waiting. He told them what a good thing it was they had done, and he told them step by step what they were going to do now that he was home. He thanked God that he was home safely and they were all together. He met and thanked their friends, fixed up the widow woman's house, held his baby girl on his lap, and promised they would be a family together: "You just watch!"

"Everybody has a special strength," Pete assured Carlos. *"Some people even have more than one. Before you give up, you have to make sure you have tried everything you know."*

"I need for you to write me a note to the teacher," Carlos said, opening his spiral to a clean sheet of white paper.

"And what do you want that note to say?" Pete asked.

"I need you to write that I was absent from school yesterday because my grandma died, and sign my mama's name to it."

Pete stared at the spiral. "I'm just not sure you want to go there."

"It worked three or four times for Joey."

"I know it did. It also got Joey a reputation. I knew a guy once who got a bad reputation, and he had a heck of a time getting rid of it."

Cricket Harrison's Reputation

In my hometown there was a fellow named Cricket Harrison. Cricket wasn't his real name. They just called him that because he had a chirpy voice like a cricket's. He also had a habit of talking on and on, just like a cricket that won't be quiet when you're trying to get to sleep at night. Cricket Harrison's best friend was a rancher named Michael Martin. Unlike Cricket, Michael was hardworking and wealthy. He managed his father's ranch and had a stable full of racing horses. Cricket worked for Michael from time to time, but mostly he liked to sit around in town at the store and talk.

One thing he liked to talk about were the secret powers he had inherited from his grandpa.

His grandfather had been known as a seer—one who could find lost objects and tell the future. Of course, Cricket only talked about such things. He never really showed any of those powers except when he got himself into debt betting on horses or playing cards. It was then he would sneak out to the Martin Ranch and steal one of Michael's best horses out of the corral. He would take that horse way out into the countryside and hide it. Then he would head back to town and wait. It never failed. After Michael Martin had searched in vain for his favorite horse, he would come to town searching for his old friend.

"Cricket!" he would exclaim when he came into the store. "I need your help. My favorite horse is missing. You know, the 'paint' horse that bred my fastest filly. I want you to use your secret powers and see if you can tell me where it is."

Cricket would close his eyes and rub his temples mysteriously. Then he would let out a big sigh. "It's no use! I can't concentrate. I have a bunch of people bothering me to pay my debts."

"Don't worry about the money," Michael assured him. "I'll take care of your bills. You concentrate on my horse."

With that, Cricket would close his eyes again, and a big smile would come over his face. "I believe I know where your horse has wandered off to. I will bring it back for you."

That trick was sort of like Joey's grandmother dying. It worked two or three times, but in the end it got Cricket Harrison into trouble. You see, Michael Martin went to Louisiana to breed his horse on a big horse farm owned by a crooked politician. While Michael was there, he heard the politician complain about the loss of a special ring that had been in his family for three generations. He had searched all over the mansion trying to find it.

"I know how to find it," Michael said. "My best friend is a 'seer.' He can tell the future and find lost objects. When my horse has been lost, he has located it two or three times. Next week when I come back to pick up my horse, I'll bring him with me. He will be able to find your ring."

The politician, who made a living outfoxing the fox, was a little skeptical. He had more reason to be skeptical the following week when Cricket arrived and immediately began denying having any secret powers. "I make some lucky guesses from time to time," said Cricket, "but I don't have any real powers."

"Maybe you can make a lucky guess about my ring," the politician said with a sly smile, hoping to expose Cricket for the fraud that he was. "I will lock you in the guesthouse for three days. By then, I'm sure, you'll be able to locate the ring."

In truth, the ring wasn't lost at all but had

been stolen by three servants who worked on the kitchen staff. They were none too happy to find out that a man of "secret powers" had been brought in to locate the ring. That very night one of those servants was told to deliver the evening meal to Cricket. The servant quietly opened the door, entered, and put the tray of food down on the table. As he was leaving, Cricket, realizing the first of his three days was gone, put his hand to the side of his face and grimaced, "Of the three, there goes the first!"

After locking the door, the servant ran to the kitchen to tell his fellow thieves. "That man! That man with the secret powers. He knows we stole the ring. As I was leaving, he looked right at me, closed his eyes, and rubbed his temples. Then he said, 'Of the three, there goes the first.' He knows we did it!"

But his friends assured him he must have misunderstood. How could he possibly know? "Don't worry," they said, "tomorrow another of us will take his food."

The next day Cricket paced in his room, worrying and fretting. If he got out of this one, he swore he would never brag again about having secret powers. He had no idea how he could find that ring! At suppertime the second of the servants brought him his food. Once again a feeling of impending doom came over Cricket. Realizing that now two of his three days were gone, he groaned and whispered, "Of the three, there goes the second."

The second servant also ran back to the kitchen. "It's true," he blurted. "Somehow he recognized me. As I was leaving the room I heard him whisper, 'Of the three, there goes the second!'"

By the end of the third day, the third servant went to Cricket's room, dropped the tray of food on the table, and threw himself on the floor to beg: "Please, we know that you know we stole the ring. Don't tell our boss. He may do more than fire us. He may fire *at* us!"

Cricket may have been lazy, but he wasn't stupid. He realized this was his chance. "I'll tell you what," he said. "Maybe there is a way out for you. While I have been here in this room, I thought I heard geese honking. Does your boss have a flock of geese?"

"Yes," the servant said. "He has a flock of

geese in his gardens."

"Listen carefully," Cricket continued. "Take the ring out into the gardens and throw it down in front of the biggest goose in the flock. Make sure the goose swallows the ring. I'll take care of the rest."

After dinner Cricket was ushered into the sitting room where the politician waited to embarrass him in front of Michael Martin. "Tell me," he asked sarcastically, "did you have any visions about my ring?"

"To be honest," Cricket replied quickly, using a term he knew little about, "while I was in your guest quarters, I had the strangest dream. I dreamt your lost ring was in the belly of the biggest goose in the flock of geese in your gardens. Do you have such a flock?"

Astounded at the nerve of this man, the politician had the biggest goose brought into the house and watched as it was killed and its stomach cut open. You can imagine his shock when the missing ring was discovered.

Cricket, for his part, was shocked at the size of the reward he received.

"I can tell you, all the way home Cricket Harrison swore he'd never again claim to have secret powers," Pete said to Carlos.

"I guess that lie got him into a mess of trouble," Carlos said thoughtfully.

"It was more than a lie. It was a reputation. A reputation is harder to get out of than a lie."

Cricket Harrison Settles a Wager

Within the month that Louisiana politician was bragging to a colleague about the amazing powers that a friend of a friend had displayed while locating a valuable piece of jewelry at his house.

"He sounds to me like a fraud. I hope you didn't give him any money," his friend said with a smirk.

"Well ... yes, I did give him a reward. At first, I thought he was a fraud. But I watched him work. I tell you, the man is a 'seer.'"

"I tell you, the only thing he could 'see' was a big sucker! He's a fraud, and you're a bigger fool than I ever imagined."

The argument continued, with neither man backing down. Finally, a large wager was made. The next week Michael Martin got an invitation to return to the politician's Louisiana horse farm with his friend Cricket Harrison. The day of their arrival they were ushered into the sitting room to be introduced. "These are my friends, Mr. Martin and Mr. Harrison. Mr. Harrison, your room is made up in the guest quarters. I thought you would need a quiet place to prepare yourself. Tomorrow morning in the gardens we will settle our wager."

The arrangement was quite simple. The politician's colleague would place an object in a box, the box would be raised to the top of the flagpole at the head of the gardens and, from the steps leading up to the main entrance, Cricket would have to identify what had been placed inside the box. It was quite simple for everyone but Cricket! He spent yet another fretful night in the guesthouse.

The next morning, to make things more complicated, the politician's colleague decided to use a small box. His plan was to put the small box inside a bigger box, and put that box inside a bigger box, and so on, until he had a great big box to hoist up the flagpole. As he prepared the boxes, he looked for something to put inside the smallest one. At that moment a little cricket hopped across the walkway in front of the flagpole. He scooped it up, shoved it into the little box, and finished his work.

Before long, Mr. Harrison was led out onto the front steps. The two politicians were with him, one on either side. Below him and above him on the steps stood half a dozen men in dark suits with sunglasses. They looked none too friendly.

The politician stated: "I bet my friend that you have the powers to identify from this distance what he has placed inside that box at the top of the flagpole."

Cricket looked toward the flagpole and then for a place to run. The men in sunglasses must have had secret powers of their own. They knew what Cricket was thinking and reached inside their suit jackets for something he didn't especially want to see. He looked back at the flagpole and began to sweat.

"Go ahead, tell him," the politician ordered Cricket. "Tell him what's in the box!"

His colleague laughed. "I told you he was a fraud." Cricket squirmed.

"Tell him!" the politician shouted. "You tell him now!"

Cricket began to stammer, "In the box ... in the box ... in the box ... "

"How did you know there is a box in a box in a box?" the colleague questioned.

But before he could reply, Cricket shook his head and stared with shame at his feet. "Oh, you poor Cricket," he murmured out loud with self-pity. "They have you trapped this time."

"I don't believe it! This man is amazing!"

"I told you he had secret powers," the politician bragged.

He gave Cricket half the winning wager and promised to be in touch with him again soon.

Cricket offered Michael Martin half his share if he would promise to convince the politician that the "seer" had moved and left no forwarding address.

Pete looked at Carlos. For the first time he felt like Carlos was measuring him to see if he were a fraud. "Hey, I was in town that afternoon when Michael Martin and Cricket Harrison came home," Pete swore. "We were giving Cricket a hard time. I remember picking up a bag filled with garbage and waving it in the air. 'Oh, great seer! Man of secret powers!' I shouted. 'Tell us what is in the bag.'

'That's a bunch of garbage!' Cricket yelled back at us. 'I have no secret powers!'

"But it was too late," continued Pete. "Cricket no longer could find any peace, even in his own home-town. In the end he really did move away, leaving no forwarding address."

"I still have a big problem," Carlos mumbled. "I was absent from school yesterday, and the teacher says if I don't bring an excuse she's going to go to my home and visit my mom."

"You haven't told me where you were," Pete said.

"Okay, if you must know. Joey skipped school. He had a whole bag of stuff with him and said he was going to go live under the channel bridge." Carlos looked at Pete defiantly. "I was worried about him. First of all, he can't swim. He can't fish either. Plus, there is a bunch of gang graffiti down under the bridge, and I don't want Joey to start hanging around with a gang."

After a long silence, Pete picked up the spiral notebook. He wrote for a minute, then handed the spiral to his young friend. Carlos read silently:

To whom it may concern:

My son Carlos was absent from school yesterday because he had to go to the eye doctor with a family friend. Our friend needed Carlos to bring him home on the bus after his examination. Thank you.

Pete had forged Carlos' mother's signature. "But what about your reputation?" Carlos asked.

"Sometimes you do what you have to do," Pete

said with a shrug. "That's what friends are for."

A Matter Between Friends

Down near the docks by the bay, Henri Boudreaux lived year round in a one-bedroom summer cottage on Juniper Street. Henri was no longer a young man; he was easily pushing seventy-five and knew he had lived the better part of his life. But he felt pretty good about that life. He was retired now, but for years and years he had trolled a shrimp boat on the bay.

Henri was a cat person. You may not know, but in this world there are cat people and dog people, and Henri was one of the former. Henri's cats always seemed happy when they came aboard Henri's shrimp boat. Even though cats hate water, they were good company once they got on the boat and found a place to be comfortable.

In the last years when Henri was still shrimping, he had found a black and white tomcat. He named it Fisher. Fisher would show up at the dock every morning, hop on board the shrimp boat, and get ready for a day of shrimping. As

Henri cranked up the diesel engine, Fisher would jump up on the engine casing and stretch out. That engine would hum and chug, and Fisher thought it was purring just for him. His nose would start to itch, and he'd stretch out and crank up his own engine. By the time they were out past the buoys, Fisher was asleep on that warm engine, dreaming of all the fish in the bay.

After Henri retired, he and Fisher would row out each morning to drown some worms. Fisher was always awarded the first catch of the day. In the afternoons they enjoyed each other's company sitting on the front porch of the cottage. Henri would sit in his rocking chair, and Fisher would jump up onto the window air-conditioning unit. When that unit kicked on and started humming, Fisher thought it was purring just for him. He'd crank up his own little engine, stretch out on that warm unit, and dream of all those fish in the bay.

Philip Evans lived two doors down and across the street from Henri in one of those big, fancy bay houses built up on stilts. At the time Philip was thirty-eight and worked in a high-dollar management position for one of the computer companies in the city. If someone had told Philip twenty years earlier, when he was in college up north, that he would be a corporate manager before he was forty, he wouldn't even have listened. When Philip Evans got out of college, he planned to change the world, and you don't do that running a corporation.

To tell the truth, Philip was still not very comfortable with how he got to be where he was at that point in his life. He did know, though, that he had made some decisions before all the facts were in and had guessed right. It was a trait his bosses admired.

Philip Evans was a dog person. Remember, in this world there are cat people and dog people, and Philip was one of the latter. Back home, the Evanses had dogs long before they had Philip. After they had Philip, they still had more dogs than you could shake a stick at. To Philip it was just natural to have a dog. So when he moved out of his apartment and into that big house by the bay, he bought a Doberman pinscher and named it Max.

As neighbors, Henri and Philip had become friends. Philip was hoping that, in their friendship, he could learn more about how Henri was so comfortable with where he was and where he had been. When Philip went over to Henri's to sit on the porch and have a cold drink, he always left Max chained up in the backyard. Max was not a cat "person."

Henri liked Philip, and he was glad for his company, but the thing Henri liked best about Philip was his wife, Marie.

"Now Marie, she is some girl, and that's fo' sho'!" Henri would say. Marie was a Cajun girl and met Philip when they were at college. Even though she worked in a tall office building downtown, she hadn't forgotten how to make a great pot of file´ gumbo. Nor had she forgotten her Southern hospitality. Henri was often invited over to enjoy the Cajun meals she prepared. When Henri went over to share the gumbo or crawfish etouffee, Fisher stayed at home. Fisher was not a dog "person."

The good news came in November. Marie found out she was pregnant. At their little celebration Philip and Marie invited Henri over and announced they wanted him to be the godfather of their baby. I'm telling you, he was delighted with the news. He couldn't quit talking about it. He came out of retirement to wander around the neighborhood telling everybody he saw that "Philip and Marie, dey gonna have a baby! And I'm gonna be de godfather!"

It was right before Thanksgiving when Philip once again amazed his bosses by making a decision before all the facts were in and guessing right. They were so excited they rewarded him with a weekend in one of those island resorts. Philip and Marie left on the evening of the first Thursday in December, flying south of the border on an unseasonably balmy day. They enjoyed themselves thoroughly and flew home on Sunday evening.

When they finally got home on Sunday night, it was well after dark. Marie went up to bed, tired but happy. Philip had to unpack and do a little work before going to bed. He was sitting at the kitchen table doing some reading when Max scratched at the back door. He opened the door and looked down, seeing that Max had once again dragged home one of his "prizes." In the past he had brought in raccoons and possums—and once a nutria, one of those big water rats that live in the banks around the bay.

I remember when my dog used to bring home prizes. She brought in rabbits and groundhogs and possums. I liked the possums best because, after a while, they got up and went away. The others I had to haul off and bury. Anyway, Max dropped the carcass on the back step, and Philip, not able to identify it, turned on the light and rolled it over with the toe of his shoe. That was when he realized it was a cat. His heart sank when he bent down to take a closer look. It wasn't just any cat. It was Fisher! Philip put his hands under the little body and carried it into the house.

That cat was dead, all right—stone cold and caked in mud. Max must have dragged that cat all over the neighborhood.

Philip took the kitchen towel and wiped at the fur on Fisher's head, wondering how he would ever be able to tell Henri what Max had done. He kept wiping away at the mud, feeling more and more heartsick. Finally, he just moved the tiny body into the sink and, using the dish rinser, washed all the mud out of the cat's fur. Philip noticed then that Max hadn't torn the cat up any ... no holes or rips. So he smoothed out the fur with his hand, and slowly an idea developed in his mind. He ran upstairs and got Marie's hair dryer and a comb.

As he blew the fur dry and combed it out, Philip thought, "Maybe if I could just sneak over there and leave Fisher on the porch. Henri will come out in the morning and find him. He'll think Fisher died in his sleep of natural causes."

So that's what Philip did. He got Fisher all dried out and brushed clean. Then he chained up Max and snuck across the street up onto Henri's porch. He laid Fisher on the window air-conditioning unit and stretched him out the way he was when he was dreaming about the fish in the bay. Philip ran back home, swearing to himself he wouldn't even tell Marie his secret.

In the morning Marie got up and got ready for the drive downtown while Philip fixed them both some breakfast. After breakfast, Marie left for work while Philip cleaned up the dishes and had some more coffee. When he went out to get in his car to go to work, he saw Henri Boudreaux standing on his front porch with the couple from the house next door. Philip backed the car out of the driveway thinking, "Now would be a good time to let myself in on the discovery. I'll stop the car, walk up the steps, and ask what happened." So that's what he did.

When he got to the top of the porch steps, Henri and his neighbors were standing around the window unit staring at Fisher. Poor Henri was shaking his head when Philip said, "Oh, no! What happened?"

Henri kept shaking his head. Philip put his hand on Henri's shoulder and repeated his question: "What happened?"

Henri looked at him, realizing for the first time that Philip had joined them. He shook his head again and said, "I don't know. It sure do beat de heck out of me, I guarantee. Ol' Fisher, he died on Friday and I buried him dere in de backyard. Uh, huh! Dis is a strange one."

Philip quietly backed down the steps, unnoticed by the little gathering on the porch. He got into his car and drove to work. On the way he began to think about the whole affair. He decided Henri had not quite got it right. Henri had called it "strange," but Philip thought that wasn't quite the right word. "Bizarre" was a better word for it.

You see, where Philip came from it wasn't strange at all for a person to try his best to keep a friend from feeling hurt. Besides, he knew all along that when you earn your living making decisions before all the facts are in, sooner or later you're going to guess wrong.

QUESTIONS: CHAPTER 7
Support Systems: Use and Abuse

The Seven Sisters' Situation

1. In a good support system each person brings his or her strengths to the group and makes the group stronger. What are the seven strengths that the girls bring to their group? How does each strength help the girls survive?

2. What strength do you bring to your family or your group? What strength would you like to have in your family or your group?

Cricket Harrison's Reputation

1. What is a reputation? Why does Pete say, "A reputation is harder to get out of than a lie"? What does that mean?

2. Is it fair the way people get their reputations?

3. What is your reputation? Do you want that reputation? How do you change a reputation?

Cricket Harrison Settles a Wager

1. Why is Cricket having such a hard time escaping his reputation?

2. In the end, Cricket must move. How does moving allow one to establish a new reputation?

3. Some people say there are only two ways to get out of a gang—die or move. If you moved to a new area, what reputation would you establish?

4. Part of what moves with you is your habits. What habits would you have to change if you wanted to change your reputation? Could you change those habits right now where you are?

5. One of the biggest issues that gets in the way of changing a reputation is a person's friends. Often friends must be changed before reputations can be changed. Would you be willing to change some of your friends to change your reputation?

A Matter Between Friends

1. Pete says at the end of the story, "You see, where Philip came from it wasn't strange at all for a person to try his best to keep a friend from feeling hurt. Besides, he knew all along that when you earn your living making decisions before all the facts are in, sooner or later you're going to guess wrong." What does Pete mean?

2. Have you ever done something to keep a friend from feeling hurt? Is it ethical to keep information from a friend?

3. When Pete writes a note to protect Carlos because Pete believes Carlos did the right thing, was that ethical? How do you feel about what Pete did?

4. Are you comfortable with making decisions before you have all the information? What factors do you consider in making decisions before you have all the information?

CHAPTER 8

Discipline: Choices and Consequences

"What do you have in the fancy envelope?" Pete asked as Carlos sat down.

"It's a note from my teacher," Carlos answered, tapping the envelope slowly on his knee. *"I'm trying to decide whether to give it to my mom."*

Pete raised his eyebrows. "You hardly ever get into trouble. What did you do?"

"That's the weird part. I'm not in trouble." He tapped the envelope again. *"It's an invitation to the awards ceremony. I'm supposed to be given the 'Discipline Honor Student' award. I got my name put on the board less than any other boy in the class."*

Pete noticed the hesitation in Carlos' voice. "I see," he said. *"A dubious distinction at best."*

"A what?" asked Carlos.

"A dubious distinction. A mixed blessing. Kind of a good and bad thing rolled up into one."

"Yeah, a dubious distinction," said Carlos slowly, seeming to enjoy the sound of the words rolling off his tongue. "It's not that I didn't try. It's just that every time I messed up, someone else messed up worse than I did! Now they want me to get up in front of the whole grade to get an award."

"I suppose I could make another appointment at the eye doctor," said Pete with a smile.

"That might be a good idea," Carlos replied.

"Would you feel better," Pete continued, "if you were receiving the 'Master of Choice' award? Or, how about the 'I Am the Man' trophy?"

"What do you mean?" Carlos spotted a story on the horizon.

"It's not about keeping your name off the board; it's about understanding that the choice belongs to you. You make the right choice, you get the right result. You make the wrong choice ... "

The Crane Wife

In a blue shack down near the docks lives an old shrimper who chooses every night to sit on a stump by the water and feed the birds. A few years back, he could be seen sitting on that stump every evening mending his nets. He always ran a one-man show: one boat, one-man crew. He was the captain, the mate, the mechanic, and the net mender. In the evenings when he wasn't mending nets, he would walk the shoreline looking for floats or pieces of netting he could use to patch his own.

One evening near sunset as he was walking along the shore, he heard the cry of a bird. Ahead on the shore he saw a crane struggling for its life. One foot was caught in some partially submerged netting. The waves continually knocked the bird to the sand as it struggled to free itself. Realizing the crane's wing had been damaged during the struggle, the shrimper approached it slowly. He took off his jacket and gently wrapped it around the bird. Freeing the tangled foot from the netting, he picked the crane up and took it back to his shack.

The shrimper bandaged the crane's wing and began to feed the bird and nurse it back to health. In time the bird regained its strength. But it never strayed far from the man's shack. Every evening when the shrimper docked his boat and returned to the shack to mend his nets, the crane would perch on the rail or the roof or the sand and keep him company. One evening in the fall the flocks of cranes were flying over the bay, heading south for the winter. The shrimper's crane looked up, called out, and flew from where it was perched on the roof. It circled the little shack two or three times, then rose and joined the migrating flock.

In the spring when the cranes returned, the shrimper thought of that bird. But he never saw a crane that flew near or perched to watch him mend his net, so in time the bird left his memory. That same autumn the shrimper fell on his boat late one afternoon while hauling in his nets. Long after sunset he managed to bring his boat to shore and steer it to the docks. There he lay until the next morning, when one of the other shrimpers found him, dragged him off his boat, and took him to the hospital. The next evening he sat in front of his shack, his leg in a cast, mending the nets he had taken in as work until he could return to his boat and the bay. As he worked he wondered how he would manage to survive the winter. He stared for a long time at the flocks of birds flying overhead on their way south. When he looked back down at the water, he saw someone walking along the shore toward him.

As the figure came closer, the shrimper saw that it was a tall, thin, and pale young woman. Her hair was a dirty blond, long and stringy, and she walked with a slight limp. For a while she stood off at a distance and watched him work. He looked up several times and smiled but said nothing. In the time it took for the sun to set, the girl approached. He soon found out she was lost and alone and had no place to stay. He told her she could spend the night there in his shack. When he finished mending and put up his nets, he limped slowly inside to fix dinner, only to find the girl had already prepared a pot of soup.

The girl stayed on and proved to be not only a good cook but also quite handy at mending nets. When the shrimper's leg began to heal, he built a room for the girl on the back of the shack. Together they managed to survive the winter and, by spring, the shrimper was up and about readying his boat for the season. He often wondered what the girl did during the day while he was working, for she never wished to go to the docks and help out on or around the boat. The end of the weekend, on Sunday night after the "Blessing of the Fleet" festival, the girl emerged from her room with a bundle in her hands. She looked wan and tired, but she smiled as she offered the shrimper a gift for the kindness he had shown her.

The shrimper undid the bundle and found inside the most beautiful netting he had ever seen. It was soft and smooth and shone in the light. It was also strong beyond belief.

She smiled as she told him, "I wove the net myself." She opened the door to her room and showed him a loom she had built. He had never thought to look in her room before, but now he knew how she had spent those days while he was working on the boat.

The following day, when he lowered that net into the water, he found it held twice the shrimp his other net held and seemed to be shaped in such a way that the shrimp rushed to fill it. Throughout the summer days his catch doubled and, even when the other shrimpers were coming in early with little to show for their work, he would come home with a full boat. That season he did so well he was able to buy another boat. The second boat did not flourish, though, even when it shadowed the first.

Over the winter the shrimper began to ask the girl if she might weave him a second net for his new boat. She knew he was doing better than he had done before and didn't understand why he needed more. But the shrimper kept begging and bothering her, so she said she would. "But you must promise not to bother me while I work," she said. "Don't ask how I'm doing, and never look into my room while I'm weaving." As she closed the door to her room, she added, "This must be the last time. Please don't ask for another net."

The shrimper kept his promise. He thought about her, and he worried about her, for she stayed in the room long periods of time. With the approach of spring and the "Blessing of the Fleet" ceremony, the girl emerged with yet another net. It was just as soft and strong as the one before, and soon both of the shrimper's boats returned each day with full catches.

It was a glorious summer. The weather was beautiful. The hurricanes passed far to the east, and the shrimper prospered. His good fortune did not go unnoticed. By fall a shrimping firm in Galveston made him an offer for his boats. It was enough, he told the girl, to build a house on the water, buy a little boat, and only have to shrimp as often as he pleased. The one catch was that the contract included an extra net, a third net, just like the special ones that came with the other two boats.

"But you promised you wouldn't ask again," the girl replied. "We agreed the second net would be the last."

He assured her this one certainly would be the last. If she would weave one more, he would never mention the nets again. The deal could not go through, he told her, without the third net.

Although she couldn't understand why he

needed the money, why he needed the third net, why he would choose to act in such a way, she finally agreed. "But you must promise not to bother me while I work. Do not ask how I'm do-ing, and never look into my room while I'm weav-ing," she warned again.

The girl retreated to her room, and the shrimper worked each day at the docks, ready-ing the boats for sale. As  winter passed and spring came, the man began to worry about the girl and about the new net. The net was needed for the sale, and the delivery date was the weekend of the "Blessing of the Fleet." Each afternoon as the weekend ap-proached, the shrimper knocked at the girl's door and asked how she was doing.

"Don't come in!" the girl cried out in a pained and thin voice. "I am working. I will be finished soon."

But will she be finished soon enough, the shrimper wondered, realizing that each day her voice seemed to be growing weaker.

On the last day of the "Blessing" weekend, concerned equally for the girl's health and his own financial future, the shrimper could wait no longer. Instead of knocking at the girl's door, he chose to open the door and step into the room. As the last light of the day shown through the little window, the shrimper looked toward the loom. There he saw, not the girl, but a large crane bent over the weaving. The crane was plucking feathers from her breast and weaving them into the net. Blood trickled down the front of the crane. The shrimper looked down and saw a line of bright red, which was woven into the last strands of the netting.

He heard a beating of wings, and felt the air rush around the room. The crane flew by his head and out the door. The shrimper stood still, his feet frozen to the floor.

"To tell you the truth," Pete said, *looking up at Carlos, "I don't know if the deal went through. I don't know what happened to the net with the blood-red streak in it—or the other nets for that matter. All I*

know is, each evening now that old shrimper sits out there on the stump in front of his blue shack and feeds the birds. It may be the only choice he has at this point. That man would still be happy if he had only chosen to follow the girl's advice and not bother her while she worked." Pete shook his head sadly.

For a minute Carlos could have believed it was Pete himself who had made the wrong choice.

Thinking again about Carlos and his invitation to the awards assembly, Pete asked, "Whose name was on the board the most times?"

"I think it was a tie. By October the teacher just left Seth's and Joey's names up there. She said there was no point in wasting the energy it took to erase them on Friday, only to put them up again on Monday morning.

"I couldn't have kept up with them if I tried," Carlos added. "Seth is just bad. But Joey never learned to take advice from the right person. Every time he *got his name on the board he would say to Seth, 'Ahh, man! It's your fault. Teacher, he told me to do it!'"*

"Sounds to me like Joey's asking the question 'Who's to blame?' instead of 'Whose choice?'"

The Gardener's Choice

I knew a man once who worked as a gardener down at the zoo. You know, when you took that field trip to the zoo, you saw people in overalls planting flowers and bushes, pulling weeds in the flower beds, arranging rocks and trees in the animal areas? Well, he was one of those guys. One day the zoo manager came to him and said, "You're in charge of the grounds this weekend. I'm taking off work for the big holiday celebration." It was one of those parade weekends. I can't remember if it was the rodeo or Martin Luther King Day or what.

Being left in charge was not the gardener's idea of a good time. "Ahh, man!" he complained to a friend. "The only reason the boss gets to go to the celebration and I don't is because I have to stay and water the plants."

"Well, I'm going," the friend said. "If you

could get someone to water the plants for you, you could go, too."

The gardener didn't want to miss any of the excitement, so he called all the monkeys together and told them, "Monkeys, I work day in and day out to make this zoo a pretty place for you to live. I have decided I need a break. I want to go to the celebration this weekend, but all the young trees and bushes in the zoo need watering. Will you water them for me while I'm away?"

"We would be glad to," answered the monkeys.

The gardener gave them the key to the shed and showed them where all the buckets and

hoses were. The following noon the head monkey got all his workers together and told them to hook up the hoses and fill the buckets. Then he said, "We must water the trees and bushes according to their needs. If they have long roots, they need lots of water. If they have short roots, they need only a little water. You must pull up the plants to see how long the roots are before you water them."

Some of the monkeys pulled up the trees and bushes, while the others measured the roots and poured water on them. Of course, an afternoon of hot sun didn't leave much life in the plants that were uprooted.

Unfortunately for the gardener, the zoo manager had to drive by the zoo on his way to the celebration, and he noticed what the monkeys were doing. He slammed on his brakes, whipped the car over, and shouted through the window, "Who told you to do that?"

"The head monkey told us," the monkeys answered.

"You go tell him the zoo manager needs to speak with him. Now!" Then he thought, if this one was chosen to be head, the rest of these monkeys must be brain-dead! The head monkey arrived, and the manager demanded, "Why did you tell these monkeys to pull up all of the young trees and bushes on the grounds?"

"Don't be angry," the head monkey

pleaded. "The gardener told us to water the little trees and bushes while he was at the celebration this weekend. If we don't know the length of their roots, how can we tell how much water to give them? Don't blame us. We were only doing our best to carry out the gardener's request."

The manager looked at the monkeys and shook his head. "I don't blame you," he said, "but I do know whom to blame."

"Later the gardener tried to put the blame on bad advice from his friend," Pete said to Carlos. "I probably don't need to tell you he got more than his name on the board. He not only lost his job, but ever since, the zoo has kept all the monkeys in cages. Did you notice that when you were on your field trip?"

Carlos smiled. "I noticed," he said.

"You still haven't given that invitation to your mom?" Pete saw the envelope sticking out of Carlos' notebook.

"It's going to be embarrassing enough. I'm afraid if my mom comes, the teacher will do something crazy, like hold me up as an example."

"How so?" Pete asked.

"Like today. The teacher got everyone's attention and said, 'I want to hold Carlos up as an example. Carlos always takes care of the little things before they become a problem.'"

Pete cringed. "What 'little things' was she talking about?"

"I don't even know," Carlos replied. "I was too embarrassed to even listen to what she said."

"For an educated woman, sometimes she doesn't know much, does she?"

"You got that right."

Pete thought for a minute, then added, "She's not far off. She just hasn't figured out the best way to let you know."

Not Our Problem

A few years back an ex-con moved in above the barbershop on Clinton Boulevard. This was back in the days when the adults ran the gangs, and the kids still did what their parents and teachers told them to do. He wasn't out of jail long before he was trying to run the whole neighborhood from right there above the barbershop. He was pretty much the boss man on Clinton Boulevard.

One afternoon he was standing up on the roof of the barbershop gazing out across the neighborhood with one of his main men. He was eating a barbecue pork sandwich. He leaned over the edge to catch a conversation on the steps below, and a big drop of barbecue sauce slid out of the side of that sandwich and dropped onto the sidewalk. He turned to his buddy and smiled. "That looks like a big old drop of blood down there," the ex-con said.

"Do you want me to go down and clean it up?" his buddy asked.

"Not our problem," he mumbled as he shoved the rest of the sandwich into his mouth and sat down to enjoy the afternoon breeze off the bay.

Nobody even noticed when a long line of ants began to make their way across the sidewalk to eat that drop of sauce.

Only a cat, half asleep in a chair in front of the barbershop, noticed when a little green lizard darted out of a flower bed and began to eat up the ants. The cat stretched, poised itself on the edge of the chair, and leapt onto the sidewalk, pinning the lizard under its paws.

Apparently, that quick movement was enough to irritate a neighborhood dog who had been sleeping in the shade underneath the shop. The dog shot out from the shade of the steps and grabbed the cat in its mouth. It was growling, the cat was howling, and instead of grabbing a hose, the cat's owner tried to break up the animals by giving the dog a swift kick in the ribs. The dog dropped the cat and went away whimpering. However, the dog's owner, a rival of our man on the roof, came running up. That's when the real fight began.

It seemed a little warm to me for all those boys to be out fighting in the street. When the dust settled, the police had six of them cuffed and leaning against the squad car. As they grabbed the ex-con and hauled him off for parole violation, the officer looked down at that dark red spot on the sidewalk and said, "Middle of the day, and you men are spilling blood on the sidewalk."

"It's not blood," the ex-con shot back. "It's barbecue sauce. I should've had him clean it up."

"Your teacher is right, don't you see?" Pete said. "Taking care of the little things is important."

Pete watched with amusement, noticing Carlos' ears perk up when he heard the ice cream truck turn onto Daniel Street. He watched Carlos join the other kids, little and big, as they gathered around the back of the truck to give their orders. Carlos never pushed to the front, but hung back, watching what other kids chose and reading and rereading the bright stickers on the side of the truck. Clutching Nutty Buddies, Rocket Pops, and Tutti-Frutti Bars, children pushed their way back out of the crowd. Last of all, Carlos stepped to the window. Even then, Pete noticed, he hadn't completely made up his mind. He asked a few questions, handed the man his money, and came back to the steps to sit down with a Fudgesicle.

He carefully unwrapped the ice cream and then began methodically licking, trying to stay ahead of the afternoon sun. "The trouble with making choices," he mumbled between licks, "is that there are so few chances—and so many things that can get in the way."

Pete smiled as he saw the chocolate ice cream beginning to gather at the corners of Carlos' mouth. "Sometimes," he said, "you're not even sure what those things are until after the choice has been made."

Fear

I came home one afternoon and found a neighbor on his hands and knees in the front yard. I would have thought he was pulling weeds, but he was too dressed up for yard work. He was reaching into the flower bed and searching in the grass.

"What's up?" I asked.

"I'm trying to find my keys."

There's nothing worse than losing your keys, so I got down on my hands and knees and began to help. We didn't experience much success. Before long, Miss Johnston came by and stopped to help, too. Then Brother Perkins lent his assistance. Mrs. Beasley was walking her little girl home from kindergarten, and they decided to join the search. As we hunted for those keys, we talked. I found out two or three things I didn't know about goings-on in the neighborhood, but we didn't find the keys.

Finally, the postman came by.

"What are you looking for?" he asked.

"We're all searching for my neighbor's lost keys," I volunteered.

"Where were you the last time you saw them?" he asked, looking at my neighbor.

We all stopped searching for a moment and turned to listen.

"The last time I had my keys I was down in the cellar checking the fuse box," he answered.

"It seems to me," the postman suggested, "you should go down in the cellar to look for the missing keys."

"I don't think so," my neighbor said. "The cellar is cold, dark, and scary. It's much better to

search for keys out here in the light of day, surrounded by my friends and neighbors."

Anger

One afternoon Reverend Johnson had scheduled an appointment with me. A political matter had come up. I can't remember now whether it was a problem with the potholes in the streets or the leaky water mains. At any rate, it was a matter on which we didn't see eye to eye.

When he got to my house, he knocked at the door and waited. Then he knocked a little louder and waited again. As you know, Reverend Johnson never minds keeping his congregation waiting for dinner  on Sunday while he finishes his sermon, but he's none too good at waiting himself. So, when I didn't answer the door after the second knock, he grabbed a piece of chalk from his pocket and wrote "Stupid Idiot" across the step. Then he turned in a huff and stalked home.

I had been across the street at Mrs. Winston's house, borrowing some coffee so Reverend Johnson and I could have a cup while we talked about the issues. Through the window I watched what was transpiring, all the while chatting with Mrs. Winston as she measured some coffee into a paper cup.

When I got home, I put my jacket on and walked over to the Reverend's house. When he opened the door, he didn't look happy to see me.

"I had forgotten the time we were to meet," I said. "I apologize that I wasn't home when you came by. Of course, I remembered everything as soon as I noticed you had left your name on my step!"

Confusion

After I got released from the army, I had to make my way back home. Sometimes I managed to get a ride, but most of the time I had to walk. One afternoon I was walking outside a small town when I saw a group of men coming toward me on the road. It was not a particularly good time or place to be walking alone. I didn't know if those men were cops or robbers, but I decided I didn't care to meet up with them and find out. I lit out across the ditch and through a field. I came to a stone wall and scrambled over it. When I dropped down on the other side, I found myself in a graveyard. That spooked me a little bit! I ran through the cemetery, dodging headstones, and looked back to see if anyone was following me. As luck would have it, there was a freshly dug grave in front of me, and I tumbled to the bottom. There I lay, quietly looking up at the rectangular patch of blue sky, wondering what my choices were now.

As it turned out, those men on the road were neither cops nor robbers. They were just a crew of county workers returning to their jobs after going into town for lunch. They watched me scramble through the ditch, across the field, and over the wall—and became curious as to the reason for my strange behavior. So they followed me.

The whole crew crossed the field and climbed over the wall into the cemetery. They wandered through the graveyard until they came to the freshly dug grave. Then they circled around and looked down into the bottom.

As soon as I saw those guys in their work clothes staring down at me, I realized my mistake. I smiled sheepishly.

There was a long silence as they stared at

me and I stared at them. Then one of them asked, "What are you doing here?"

"In this world," I replied, "we are always hoping for simple answers to complex questions. Oftentimes, though, the answer depends on your point of view. In this case, I can safely say that I am here because of you, and you are here because of me."

Pete looked at Carlos and grinned. Carlos had taken the invitation out of his notebook and was again tapping it against his knee. "So," Pete asked, "what are you going to do with that envelope?"

"I've been thinking," Carlos answered. "My teacher has come to school nearly every day this year, even when she had to ride the bus. The class next to us has a sub almost every week. If she wants me to give this invitation to my mom, then I guess I ought to give it to her."

Carlos got up from the step. "Besides, maybe my mom will decide not to come. I don't know what makes that crazy teacher think our mamas can skip work just to see us get some goofy award."

QUESTIONS: CHAPTER 8
Discipline: Choices and Consequences

The Crane Wife

1. The shrimper chooses to help the crane by repairing its wing and taking care of it until it is well. Why was this a good choice?

2. The crane chooses to repay the shrimper by making the shrimper nets that double his catch. But the shrimper wants more and more. He doesn't know that each net takes a physical toll on the girl. In the <u>Merchant of Venice</u>," a play by William Shakespeare, the merchant wants the "pound of flesh closest to the heart." What does that mean?

3. What choice have you made that cost you "a pound of flesh closest to (your) heart"? Has someone done something for you that cost him or her a "pound of flesh"?

4. Why does the shrimper go from being a giver to being a taker? Why does he have to lose what he loves before he can be a giver again? Do you know someone who is only a taker? Do you know someone who is a giver? What are you? Can a person be both?

5. Why do our choices define who we are?

The Gardener's Choice

1. Many individuals blame other people for their choices. In this story, who blamed whom?

2. Do you blame others for your choices? Why or why not?

3. If you blame others for your choices, you have given them power over your life. Why is this true?

4. What can you say to yourself when you make a bad choice?

5. Are there individuals who never make bad choices?

Not Our Problem

1. How does not "taking care of the little things" add up to a big problem? Can you give an example?

2. When people say, "It's not my problem," what are they really saying?

3. When you live with other people, must you sometimes be responsible for, or help with, problems you didn't create? Why or why not?

Fear

1. Why is the unknown more frightening than the known?

2. Why do we try to find answers from what we know rather than seek answers from areas with which we aren't as familiar?

3. How does your fear keep you from getting certain jobs? Talking to certain people? Getting educated?

Anger

1. How does anger interfere with good decision-making? Why do some people allow anger to make choices for them?

2. People often get angry because they're afraid. The last time you were angry, what were you afraid of?

3. When people get angry, the little voice inside their heads give them a "should" or "ought" message. For example, she "should be at home" or he "should show me respect." The last time you were angry, what was the "should" message inside your head? Would there have been a reason why the other person might have needed to do what he or she did?

Confusion

1. Sometimes choices get made because the interpretation of the situation is wrong or the person is simply confused. The last time you were confused by something, how did you make your decision?

2. Pete says, "Oftentimes, though, the answer depends on your point of view." What does that mean?

3. What can you do when a situation is confusing?

CHAPTER 9

About Instruction:
Knowing and Learning

Pete watched the kids coming home and realized it was the last day of the school year. They were full of talk about report cards, next year, and especially summer vacation. Some kids looked like they had just been released from prison, while others were disappointed they had to wait a week before summer school started. It was quite a while after that first wave of students before Pete saw Carlos slowly making his way down the sidewalk. He was trying to watch the stone he was kicking as he used both hands to lug a grocery bag filled with his school papers and supplies. He gave the stone one last kick, then flopped down on the step.

"I passed fifth grade," he announced. "Next year I'll ride the bus to junior high."

"So they managed to teach you everything you need to know to go on to the big school on the highway?" Pete asked.

"I'm not so sure," Carlos replied as he rustled through the grocery bag searching for his report card. He pulled it out and studied it for a long time. "It seems I know a whole lot of important stuff. I also know I spend a lot of time learning stuff at school. I'm just not sure it's the same stuff. I'm not even sure what this means," he said, pointing at the card. "Most of the time we're talking in the same language, but we're not talking about the same things."

"I think I hear what you're saying," said Pete. "I had an uncle who was deaf as a post."

Uncle Kenneth's Axe Handle

When I first left home and came to this town, it was because my Uncle Kenneth lived here with his wife and children. He worked a little land out on the peninsula. He had a few animals, but mostly he made his living taking people back and forth across the ship channel in a small boat. As he began to lose his hearing, his family took advantage of him. They spent more money than he could make and, over time, he got further and further into debt.

One day when his wife was in town, she heard that the sheriff was going to pay a visit and try to repossess some of their things. She rushed home and, in a very loud voice, told her husband  that she and the children would leave the house—and he should figure out what to tell the sheriff.

Off they went, leaving my Uncle Kenneth on the porch to figure out what to say to "the man." Uncle Kenneth got a good long piece of driftwood, sat on the porch, and began to think and whittle.

He thought, That sheriff is going to come up to me, take one look and ask, "What are you whittling?"

I'll look up and say, "An axe handle."

He'll ask, "How long is it going to be?"

So I will point right here and tell him, "Right up to this knot."

He'll say, "Where's your ferry boat?"

I'll tell him, "I tarred her up, and she's lying on the shore cracked at both ends."

"Well then, where is your mare?" he'll ask.

"She's out in the stall, big with foal," I'll reply.

Then he'll ask, "How about your cow and the cow shed?"

I'll tell him, "That's not far away. If you climb the hill, you are there in no time."

Satisfied that his conversation with the sheriff would go well, my Uncle Kenneth commenced to whittling on the stick. In the meantime, the sheriff planned to meet his deputy at Kenneth's at one o'clock in the afternoon. The sheriff came in by the main road from the county seat. The deputy was coming from another job and had stopped at an icehouse on the bay road to get a bite to eat.

The sheriff waited by the road for his deputy but eventually decided to go on up and talk with Kenneth alone. When he got out of the car, he could see my Uncle Kenneth sitting in front of the house.

"Good day to you," the sheriff said, stepping up onto the porch.

"It's an axe handle," my uncle replied.

"How far is it up the road to the icehouse?" the sheriff asked.

Kenneth pointed to the stick. "Oh, about right up here to this knot," he said.

The sheriff was a bright fellow and understood the conversation was going nowhere. He looked at his papers a second and then asked, "Where is your old lady?"

"I tarred her up, and she's lying down on the shore cracked at both ends."

"Well then, where is your daughter?" the sheriff asked, equal parts confused and irritated.

"She's out in the stall, big with foal."

By this time the sheriff realized the time he had wasted coming out to talk with my Uncle Kenneth. "You go to the devil, you old fool!" he said, turning to walk back to his car.

My Uncle Kenneth smiled and pointed up beyond the house. "That's not far away," he said. "If you climb the hill, you are there in no time."

Carlos laughed. "That's how it is sometimes at school. The teacher will look confused and tell us we need to be on the right page. 'Everybody needs to turn to page 182.' We all look down to check, and we _are_ on page 182!"

Carlos was quiet for a bit, and then he said, "That's why I wonder if I'll know enough when I get to junior high."

"That _is_ a worry," Pete responded. "A person can get in a mess of trouble if he heads off on important business without knowing all he needs to know." Pete stretched his legs to get comfortable. "You know, one of Miss Wilson's chicken eggs hatched, and a little chick was trying to survive in Miss Wilson's backyard."

"Not easy to do," Carlos noted. "I believe there's still a big old mess back there from when you fixed her roof."

"Yes, but at least the Wilsons' roof is no longer falling down on their heads. The little chick had concerns of a different nature."

The Sky Is Falling

One day a little chick slipped through the fence and out onto the sidewalk. A delivery truck roared by on its way to the Main Street grocery. The noise of the truck alone might have frightened that little bird to death, but when the truck hit a pothole, the whole street shook. When the whole street shook, a small piece of mortar rattled loose from the bricks in the building and came down with a thump right on top of that little chick's head.

"Oh, my gosh," the chick said, "the sky is falling!" She raced off to tell the other birds. "The sky is falling! The sky is falling!" she cried as she ran along the fence.

Miss Wilson's big hen came fluttering out of her tin roost. "What's that? What's that?" she clucked. "The sky is falling?" She looked up at the blue beyond.

"Yes," said the chick. "A piece of it fell and hit me right here on the head."

The hen saw a bump on the chick's head and assumed the worst. She flew up over the fence and joined the cry of alarm.

"The sky is falling!" they shouted as they

302

bustled through the vacant lot.

A warty Muscovy duck had waddled up from the city park. He was so fat from the crumbs left behind by the park visitors that he had long since forgotten anything he once knew about flight and the sky. "The sky is falling?" he asked with alarm in his voice.

"Yes! A piece of it hit this little chick in the head."

"We better tell the others!" the duck said, leading the parade of alarmists toward the park.

"The sky is falling! The sky is falling!" the threesome shouted as they entered the park.

"What's that?" the formerly wild goose said, looking up from her search for bugs amid the park litter. "I knew someday this would happen. One more entitlement down the drain." The goose joined the wild chase.

Coyote, the last of the country folk to move to the city, was lurking in the woods by the park. As the fearful feathered foursome passed close by, he heard the hen cry, "We must find a safe haven or we shall all die!"

"Haven or heaven," the others chimed in. "The sky is falling! The sky is falling!"

With that, the sly coyote stepped out and said, "I know just the place. Quick, follow me!" He headed through the woods toward the highway. Those foolish birds were so excited they never thought to compare catastrophes. They followed Coyote into the woods and out by the highway, where Coyote pointed to a dark round culvert. "The sky can't fall on you in there," he shouted, looking skyward with mock alarm. He moved aside to let the three plump fowl and the little chick step into the darkness. Then, licking his chops, he turned to follow.

At that very moment, the same grocery

truck that had loosened the mortar that sent the birds scurrying swerved on the highway to avoid yet another pothole. A crate of potatoes became airborne and landed with a thud on the hungry coyote. The little chick, watching from the dark culvert, looked up fearfully toward that circle of blue sky. Turning toward the other birds she said, "Move farther back. It's worse than I thought!"

"I believe if you were to walk down to the highway," Pete said, looking up toward the clear blue sky, "you might still find those crazy birds. A little bit of knowledge applied without reason can lead folks to a dark end."

"I can see that," Carlos said. "What I can't see is how a person can be sure he knows enough."

"If a person can't see, it's hard to know enough." Carlos could tell by Pete's smile that another story was coming. He leaned back against the steps and waited. Carlos was on summer vacation now. He knew he had time enough for all the stories Pete wanted to tell.

The Blind Dixie Gospel Quartet Meets the King of the Circus

Some years ago I had a job as a roustabout for a circus. I was with the crew that came into town ahead of the circus to set things up. I worked during the circus taking tickets and cleaning up after the animals and the customers, and I took the tents down when it was time to leave town. We went into a town once to set up, and I happened to meet a gospel group. It was a quartet of men who could sing like canaries, but each was blind as a bat. We started talking, and when they found out I was with the circus, they got all worked up.

"Can you introduce us to an elephant?" one of them asked.

"That would be wonderful," another added. "We've heard people tell about an elephant, but we can't imagine."

"Yes, sir, we would love to see an elephant," a third one said, and they all laughed.

I led them a couple of blocks so they would be on the parade route from the train station to the circus grounds. I told them to wait right there. Before noon the circus parade would pass, and I would try to introduce them to an elephant.

Sure enough, as the parade came by, those four blind men were standing in the sunshine on that corner waiting and smiling. One of the handlers stopped our biggest elephant right in front of those four men. The shadow of the beast darkened the street corner, and they could feel the elephant's presence.

The first man found the curb with his cane and stepped into the street. Reaching out, he grabbed hold of the elephant's trunk, and the elephant curled his trunk right around the man. Startled, he stumbled back onto the sidewalk.

The second man stepped down and reached out, grabbing hold of the elephant's ear. He felt it as it flopped back and forth.

The third man reached up and felt the elephant's side, running his hands back and forth against the rough hide.

The last man grabbed ahold of the elephant's tail, tugging on it several times before letting go.

As the parade moved down the street, the men listened and smiled, happy they now knew about the elephant. Later that day, however, an argument broke out among them as to the true nature of an elephant.

The first man said, "I was surprised to find the elephant so much like a snake. When it began to coil around me, I was scared half to death."

"That's ridiculous," the second man said. "The elephant is not at all like a snake. The elephant is much more like a fan. I felt it—thin and flat and waving about. I felt the air stirring around me."

"A snake? A fan?" the third man said in amazement. "I don't know how you could have missed him. The elephant is like a wall. A huge, rough wall. He was so big, I could not have walked around him."

"Big?" the fourth man said. "I hardly think so. Why, I had both my hands around him and could have pulled him up on the sidewalk had I cared to. An elephant is more like a rope than a wall or fan or snake."

Those four men argued about the elephant the rest of the day. By nighttime, three of the men fell asleep in silence and anger. But the fourth lay awake thinking about the sounds and smells of that circus parade. He thought about the cool shadow the elephant cast on their street corner. He tried to imagine an animal that could be at once a snake and a fan and a wall and a rope. He felt, again, the sidewalk tremble as the elephant walked away. When he closed his eyes and went to sleep, he dreamt that he was leading the parade, riding atop the magnificent elephant, king of the circus.

"It's important to trust what you know," Pete said, "but you also have to be willing to trust what other people know and try to make sense of it."

Carlos had a strained look on his face. "Why is learning so complicated?" he asked.

"Learning can be more than complicated. At times it's downright painful."

Turtle Learns to Fly

"Every year in autumn the migrating ducks stop off for a rest over on West Bay. Remember when we walked down there last fall and looked out at that huge flock?"

Carlos nodded. He could still see that "V" in the sky, circling, then settling on the water.

Well, there was a certain turtle who lived down on West Bay and always looked forward to the arrival of those ducks. The turtle wanted to hear all about their travels—where they had been, what they had seen, and where they were headed. Each year he thought how wonderful it would be to fly.

"I wish I could fly," he said to his friends. "If I could fly, I would go south with the ducks to the warm weather and the beaches. I could look down and see the whole world."

"Why don't you just shut your trap," the other turtles told him. "Turtles can't fly, and we don't want to hear any more about it."

But he couldn't shut his trap. The more he thought about flying, the more excited he became. He talked and talked about it.

One year, when the ducks arrived and he heard their travel adventures, Turtle could stand it no longer.

"When you fly south this year, I'm going with you," he said. "The others all tell me turtles can't fly. But I have a plan." To his surprise, the ducks not only listened to his plan but also promised to help. Turtle was so excited he couldn't eat or sleep. "Those other turtles will be so amazed," he thought, "when they see me soaring above them in the sky."

When the ducks were ready to venture on, Turtle arrived with a long, thin stick. Just as they had planned, two ducks swam forward and took up the stick, each holding an end in its bill. Turtle

clamped onto the stick in the middle, ready to fly. "Remember," the lead duck cautioned, "don't let go of the stick. With no feathers on your shell, I'm afraid your landing would not be light and graceful."

"I'll remember," Turtle mumbled, the stick clenched tightly in his jaws.

The ducks rose from the surface of the bay and circled up and up into the sky. Turtle could not believe his eyes. There was the shore! There was the bay! There were the boats ... and the bridge ... and the town! He was flying! He imagined the amazement and envy of the other turtles. He looked back down toward his home and saw the other turtles, but they didn't see him! They weren't looking up in the air.

"What good is flying," he thought, "if no one sees me?" With that thought, he began to wave his little turtle legs and shout, "Hey, look at me! I'm flying!"

The moment he opened his mouth he began his long, not-so-graceful descent to the water's surface. The turtle landed with a smack, right on his shell, cracking it to pieces.

"Ouch!" said Carlos, grimacing.

"Yes, sir!" Pete replied. "And every turtle since has had those same cracks all over its shell. They serve as a reminder that turtles are not supposed to

fly. Some lessons can be pretty painful. I knew a young man once who fell almost as far as that turtle."

Carlos looked up. "Did he live?"

"You might call it that. This kid fell so deeply in love, he had trouble coming up for air."

Wisdom or Air?

There was a young man who lived over on Fifth Street and thought he was God's gift to the world. And in some ways he was. He was the star of the football team, the fastest runner on the track team, and the slickest hustler in the pool hall. The girls buzzed around him like mosquitoes after a summer rain, but he wouldn't be satisfied until he won the heart of the only girl not interested in him.

She was a new girl who had moved into the neighborhood, and she had never seen him carry a football or win a hundred-yard dash. "Those things may seem important," she said, "but I'm looking for a man who is wise."

"Then I will learn to be wise," the young man replied.

Someone must have told him Mr. P.G. Green knew something about wisdom, because the next thing you know that fellow was standing right on the doorstep at the corner of Ella and Hawthorne.

"I have come to learn wisdom," he announced.

"To get wisdom you must want it more than anything else in the world," Mr. Green told him.

The boy thought for a moment about that beautiful girl who expected him to be wise. He got a little swimmy-headed just thinking about her. "Yes, sir," he told Mr. Green. "I want wisdom more than anything else in the world!"

"Then I will give you your first lesson," Mr. Green replied. "Come with me."

Mr. Green led the young man to the back of the house and instructed him to put his hands in the back pockets of his jeans and kneel down in front of a washtub filled with rainwater.

"Look long and hard at your reflection in the water," said Mr. Green.

When the boy bent down to look, Mr. Green shoved his head into the tub and held it under the water until the young man was half drowned. At last he let loose his grip, and the boy came up sputtering and coughing.

"Tell me what you were thinking about when your head was under the water."

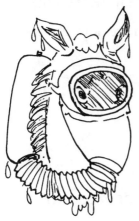

"Tell you what I was thinking about?!" the boy sputtered in disbelief. "I was thinking, 'If I don't get some air, I'm going to drown.'"

"Are you sure? You didn't think about scoring touchdowns or winning races or impressing women?"

"No," the boy answered. "I thought only about air."

"Mark that down as your first lesson," Mr. Green said. "When you want wisdom as much as you wanted air, then you will be a wise man."

That afternoon the young man went to see his girl.

"Did Mr. Green teach you how to be wise?" she asked.

He looked down at the sidewalk and kicked a stone into the street. "He only gave me my first lesson. He taught me that air is more important than wisdom. I'm afraid I will be older than Mr. Green before I'm ready to be wise."

Seeing that the young man had learned both honesty and humility in one short lesson, she smiled a smile that made his heart do a flip. "I believe I will hang around and see how the second lesson goes," she commented.

He only hoped the second lesson would not be quite as difficult.

"Joey got one of those painful lessons last week," Carlos said, looking over at Pete with a small grin and a shake of the head.

"Tell me how that happened," Pete said.

Carlos took a deep breath and began slowly.

"You know, Joey finally got a whipping in the principal's office. A bunch of us were messing around the day we had a substitute teacher. After she gave us a warning, only Joey kept it up. He was pretty funny, too. Every time the teacher turned to write something on the board, Joey would stand up at his

316

seat, watch her closely, and do everything she did. Only he did it great big and silly."

"Then he got caught?" Pete asked.

"Oh, yeah. He got caught all right."

Joey Meets the Board of Education

Instead of watching the teacher, Joey was watching Ivy Johnson to see if she was laughing

at him. When he got to the principal's office, he started into his usual routine—though I think he must have realized right away that he was in big trouble. Every other time this year that he had been to the office he told the principal he had to call his Grandma Ford before he could get a whipping. The principal would call his grandma, and Grandma Ford would come up to the office. She would burst into the office fussing like crazy at Joey and apologizing to the school for his behavior. Then she would grab him by the ear—or by the hair at the nape of his neck.

Joey said when she did those things it always made the people in the office nervous.

"Maybe this is something you need to take care of at home," they would suggest to Joey's grandma. Each time she assured them she would. Then she would march Joey right out of the school and back to the house.

"Go break a switch off the tree," she would order.

Joey always took his time. Sometimes it took two or three trips before he got the right-size stick.

"By then," Joey said, "she wasn't quite as mad."

Joey's grandma was sick most of the year, and she knew she was dying. I don't think she really had her heart in Joey's punishment. After she finished, Joey said she would send him to his room. Before long, Joey would smell cornbread cooking in the oven. Cornbread is his favorite.

There we were up at school, and Joey was at home eating cornbread and watching TV with his grandmother.

Joey's grandma died in April. So last week

when he went to the office, things were different.

Joey used his usual line: "You can't whip me unless you call home first."

The office lady called home, and Joey's mother came to school. She looked at Joey, and she looked at the principal. "I guess you're going to have to give that boy a whipping. His grandma is gone now, and he has to learn to behave himself."

When Joey came back to the class, he was smiling like it didn't hurt. But you could tell, when he sat down, it must have hurt a little.

Pete rubbed his backside and winced. "I bet his mother had cornbread waiting for him when he got home."

Carlos just shook his head. "I hope he learned his lesson. At junior high they don't give pops. At junior high they put you out of school. Joey doesn't need to be put out of school."

319

QUESTIONS: CHAPTER 9
About Instruction: Knowing and Learning

Uncle Kenneth's Axe Handle

1. Teaching is outside the head. Learning is inside the head. Why are Uncle Kenneth and the deputy having such difficulty communicating?

2. Is it possible to know something and not be able to share that knowledge?

3. One of the reasons for communication is to share meaning and information. In order to share meaning, there must be some common understandings. Uncle Kenneth is working from a previous conversation he'd had inside his head. How can a conversation inside your head affect your communications with others?

The Sky Is Falling

1. "A little bit of knowledge applied without reason can lead folks to a dark end." What does that mean?

2. The chick took one incident and interpreted it against her frame of reference. Every individual sees the world through a lens that includes and excludes data. Part of learning is to get as much of the data as possible. Often the data excluded are as important as the data included. For example, the chick excludes the truck, the noise because of the pothole, etc. What incident has happened to you or someone you know in which part of the data was not examined before a conclusion was reached?

3. What could the chick have done to gather all the data?

The Blind Dixie Gospel Quartet Meets the King of the Circus

1. Why does each member of the gospel quartet have such a different description of the elephant?

2. In order to learn, people must make meaning inside their heads and communicate with what is outside their heads. To do that, individuals have structures inside their heads (schema) that store and organize data. Each of these men stores data based on an association with something they already know. For example, one states that the elephant is like a snake. Some people store data on the basis of how something feels (tactile). Some people store data on the basis of how something makes them feel (emotion). When you want to remember something, what do you do?

3. How could these men have gotten a better idea of what an elephant is?

4. A teacher can make a big difference in learning when he or she points out the key pieces of anything to be learned and tells why those pieces are important for understanding. If you were teaching these men about the elephant, what would they need to know in order to understand what an elephant is?

5. When a person doesn't have a teacher who can point out the key pieces to be learned, how can that person learn

it? How did the one member of the quartet arrive at the best "picture" of an elephant?

Turtle Learns to Fly

1. Experience is also a teacher. What did the turtle learn from his flying experience?

2. If turtle goes flying again, what does he need to remember?

3. To learn anything, there is a period of time when an individual is a novice, a beginner. When a person is a beginning learner, he or she has no experience to use to make judgments, so he or she must follow basic rules. Why did the turtle have such a hard time with this?

4. At the end of the story, Pete says turtles were never meant to fly—yet turtle did! The Wright brothers flew the first airplane, even though almost everyone at the time said it wasn't possible for humans to fly. What have you (or someone you know) done that was supposed to be impossible?

5. Learning can sometimes be painful. Why? What learning experience have you had that was painful? Some individuals are afraid to learn something new because they might be embarrassed. How does that fear keep them stuck where they are?

6. Sometimes individuals don't want other individuals to learn because they're afraid they'll lose them. When people get educated, they often leave the neighborhood. Do you

know someone who has gotten an education and then left the neighborhood? Do you know anyone who is afraid that an education will mean needing to leave the neighborhood?

Wisdom or Air?

1. What did Mr. Green mean when he said, "When you want wisdom as much as you wanted air, then you will be a wise man"?

2. How does the ego sometimes get in the way of learning?

3. The research on learning notes when someone learns something, his or her perception of self is changed. In other words, learning changes personal identity. If your identity is being a fighter and a lover, are there some things you must not learn in order to keep your identity? If your identity is being a caretaker and a rescuer, are there some things you must not learn in order to keep your identity?

4. In early learning, there is a loss of control. We are often dependent upon outside help and information. Why does that outside dependence sometimes bother people?

5. What is something you would like to learn, but have fears about not being successful?

Joey Meets the Board of Education

1. In elementary school, when a student chooses not to learn, there is often punishment. What happened to Joey?

2. Carlos is afraid that when Joey gets to junior high school, the principal will tell him to leave if he misbehaves. In other words, Joey will lose the opportunity to learn. What happens to people when the chance to learn is taken away?

3. For many adults, going back to school is very difficult. Why?

4. For many students, school is not a place to learn. It is a place to find boyfriends or girlfriends. It is a place to meet and see friends. For many students, school is an awful experience. Why?

5. What could Joey do to still have fun and yet learn? Is that possible?

6. How can a person who hates school still learn while he or she is in school?

EPILOGUE

Story Roots

Late in the summer, Carlos looked up after one of Pete's stories and asked, "How is it that you always have the right story to tell at just the right time?"

"Well," Pete answered, "let me tell you a story."

The Perfect Shot

In town when I was growing up, there was a man who had gotten himself crosswise with the law. He had been charged several times with some gun-related crimes and had to give all his guns to the sheriff or go to jail. This fellow had been the best hunter in the area, always bringing in the biggest deer, the most ducks, you name it. So when he got his guns taken away he decided to learn how to hunt with a bow and arrow. That man spent hours learning how to shoot with a bow, and sure enough, after a few years he had once again become the best hunter in the area, and without ever having to shoot a gun. He was very cocky about his newfound skill, even claiming to be the best marksman with a bow and arrow since the time of the Comanche.

One afternoon he was out hunting and came over a little rise. There in front of him was a wooden shed. On the side of the shed were eight or ten targets. Dead center, in the bull's-eye of each target, was a single arrow. The hunter stared at those targets for a long time, realizing somewhere nearby was a marksman whose skill was even greater than his own.

"I've got to find out who shot those arrows," he said out loud. "Surely he knows some secret I have yet to discover. If he were to share his secret with me, I could be even better with the bow."

He set off to find the man who shot the arrows into those targets. He soon discovered it was not a man at all who had shot those arrows, but a young boy about your age and size.

Carlos stared at Pete without blinking, hanging on each word of the story.

The hunter walked with the boy around to the back of the shed and pointed at the targets.

"I need to know your secret. How is it that you were able to do this?"

"It's really simple," the boy replied. "I stood right back there on the road and, after aiming carefully, shot each of those arrows. Then I came up to the shed and painted a target around the spot where each arrow hit."

Carlos let out a deep breath.

Pete smiled. "Ever since I was a little boy, I loved to listen to stories," he said. "They are everywhere! They unfold all around us each day. I just pay atten-

tion—and wait for the good ones. When I hear one, I tell it over to myself, then put it away for safekeeping. Now I have so many I can take just about any moment and paint a story around it."

ROOTS OF THE STORIES

CHAPTER 1
Tales of Poverty and Wealth

Think Rather of Zebra: a Sufi tale offered by California storyteller Sunwolf on the Internet.

The Remarkable Dreams of Rufus Burns: "The Peddler's Dream," an English folktale found in Jane Yolen's <u>Favorite Folktales from Around the World</u>, and <u>The Journey</u>, a Jewish folktale by Uri Shulevitz, are both examples of this wonderful story. I published a version, "The Unremarkable Dreams of Tommy Chapman," in the collection <u>Short Tales, Tall Tales, and Tales of Medium Stature</u>. I have enjoyed a variety of versions from storytellers Elizabeth Ellis, Tom McDermott, Jeannine Pasini-Beekman, and others.

The Millionaire: a traditional Rom (gypsy) tale from a Martin Heidegger collection, referred to me on the Internet by Colorado storyteller Christopher Maier.

328

Miss Thornton's Poor Sister: "The Poor Farmer," a version of a German folktale collected by the Brothers Grimm; appears in Stories for the Telling, by William R. White.

Willie, the Shoeshine Man: an adaptation of "The Sword of Wood," a Jewish folktale told by Boston storyteller Doug Lipman, found in Best Loved Stories Told at the National Storytelling Festival.

CHAPTER 2
The Role of Language and Story

The Argument in Signs: a Jewish folktale found in Favorite Folktales from Around the World, edited by Jane Yolen. A Zen version of this tale may be found in the compilation by Paul Reps titled Zen Flesh, Zen Bones; it is also on Chicago storyteller Syd Lieberman's tape Joseph the Tailor and Other Jewish Tales under the title "The Debate in Sign Language." It appears in written form in More Best Loved Stories Told at the National Storytelling Festival.

The Barn Is Burning: a version of this wonderfully humorous story can be found in Afro-American Folk Tales: Stories from the Black Tradition, edited and selected by Roger Abrahams.

The Family Tradition: a version of a traditional Jewish Bal Shem Tov tale, this is a favorite of storytellers. I have been moved by simple and powerful versions of this tale told by both Jeannine Pasini-Beekman and Galveston's Rabbi Jimmy Kessler.

CHAPTER 3
Referring to Resources

Common Sense: a version of this Ananzi (also Anansi and Aunt Nancy) tale appears on Len Cabral's cassette <u>Ananzi</u>.

A Dozen Kernels of Corn: based on a conversation over the Internet with storyteller Miriam Nadel about a traditional folktale from India of a king who gives each daughter a grain of wheat.

One Whisker from the Wild Dog: versions of this tale include "The Lion's Whisker" and "The Tiger's Whisker," both of which are traditional folktales from Africa and Asia.

The Single Flame: one of many Nasrudin Hoja tales adapted for Pete's telling. A version of this story, "Hoca and the Candle," appears in the Barbara Walker collection titled <u>Watermelons, Walnuts, and the Wisdom of Allah</u>. An Ethiopian folktale version titled "Fire on the Mountain" was shared over the Internet by Jane Kurtz of North Dakota.

Getting Out of a Load of Trouble: heard as part of an acceptance speech told by Norma Livo at the National Storytelling Conference in Philadelphia, July 1996.

Spread Your Fingers When You Eat: the story "Spreading Fingers for Friendship" can be found in <u>Afro-American Folk Tales: Stories from the Black Tradition</u>, edited and selected by Roger Abrahams.

The Bleacher Bum: adapted from an angel story collected by Sophie Burnham and heard in a speech at the National

Storytelling Conference in Atlanta, July 1995.

Carlos and the Flying Boat: an adaptation of a traditional Jack tale, collected by Richard Chase and found in <u>The Jack Tales</u>. The characters appear in many story formats around the world, including <u>The Adventures of Baron Von Munchausen</u>. My adaptation borrows freely from the telling of "Jack and the Magic Boat," by Philadelphia storyteller Ed Stivender. The story can be found in <u>More Best Loved Stories Told at the National Storytelling Festival</u>, as well as Ed's cassette tape <u>The Juggler of Notre Dame and Other Miracle Stories</u>.

CHAPTER 4
Hidden Rules Among Classes

Cousin Jimmy's Dilemma: adapted from an original story by Dr. Ruby Payne.

An Experiment in Distance Learning: another favorite among storytellers. The teacher is often a village storyteller or "griot" in the African setting.

The Alley Cat's Secretary of State: adapted from a Shan tale from Burma titled "Tiger's Minister of State" from the Harold Courlander collection <u>The Tiger's Whisker and Other Tales from Asia and the Pacific</u>.

The Dogs Choose a President: part of the Pete dialogue; based on a Lakota Sioux story pointed out to me by storyteller Bob Kanegis over the Internet.

A Vest Pocket Full of Beef: a traditional tale told in many cultures, including Jewish and Nasrudin Hoja (Arab) versions. A Jewish version can be found in Jane Yolen's <u>Favorite Folktales from Around the World</u>; the Nasrudin tale appears in <u>Stories of the Spirit, Stories of the Heart</u>, edited by Christina Feldman and Jack Kornfield.

If Only You Would Flatter: also embedded in the Pete dialogue, this is a Nasrudin tale, a version of which appears in <u>Stories of the Spirit, Stories of the Heart</u>.

CHAPTER 5
Spring Break: A Leisurely Look at the Characteristics of Generational Poverty

The Woman in the Blue House on Oak Street: Jesus' parable of the prodigal son, one which I have found to be the most distressing to middle-class sensibilities, found in the Gospel of Luke, Chapter 15.

Little Eight John: an African-American tale of warning for children, found in a number of collections, including <u>Afro-American Folk Tales: Stories of the Black Tradition</u>, edited and selected by Roger Abrahams. Storyteller Cynthia Lockwood of Houston, Texas, introduced me to this one.

The Eagle Chick: adapted from <u>Stories of the Spirit, Stories of the Heart</u>. Washington, D.C., storyteller Rex Ellis found this to be one of the most disturbing and hopeless of Pete's tales.

In Whose Hands Is the Fate of the Army? a version is found in Stories of the Spirit, Stories of the Heart.

The Story of Coach 'Stump' Barnes: an original tale, based on many like it that I have heard throughout my lifetime. Stories of people succeeding against the odds inspire success. People can't hear enough of these stories.

Looking for Paradise: a version of this Jewish folktale, "Could This Be Paradise?" was told by Steve Sanfield, a California storyteller and author, at the National Storytelling Festival. It was published in Best Loved Stories Told at the National Storytelling Festival.

A Bird in the Hand: another traditional folktale found on California teller Milbre Burch's cassette In the Family Way.

CHAPTER 6
Role Models, Emotional Resources, and Decision-Making

A Million Ideas: based on a Ukrainian folktale. Mary Hamilton, a Louisville, Kentucky, storyteller, has a version on her tape of folktales, "100 Ideas and Then Some." Tom McDermott, of Fort Worth, tells a version in song.

Strength: a Limba tale from West Africa, found in Margaret Read McDonald's collection of stories titled Peace Tales: World Folktales to Talk About. Providence, Rhode Island, storyteller Len Cabral tells a version of this tale.

Joey Brings Home His Pay: a traditional folktale, versions of which appear in many cultures, including this Jack tale titled "Lazy Jack," an English story found in Jane Yolen's <u>Favorite Folktales from Around the World</u>.

The Best Thief: another traditional folktale first heard as a Hispanic story told and published by Arizona bilingual storyteller Joe Hayes in his collection <u>The Day It Snowed Tortillas: Tales from Spanish New Mexico</u>. My daughter, Elena, collected an Irish version of this tale from Batt Burns, who told it to her in Sneem, County Kerry, during the summer of 1993. It is included on his cassette <u>Irish Tales for Young and Old</u>.

The Gardener's Son's Quest: a traditional Irish folk/fairy tale adapted from William Butler Yeats' <u>Irish Fairy and Folk Tales</u>.

CHAPTER 7
Support Systems: Use and Abuse

The Seven Sisters' Situation: an original tale. I gave each girl a coping mechanism often absent among people who grow up in the culture of poverty.

Cricket Harrison's Reputation and *Cricket Harrison Settles a Wager*: adapted from "The Cricket" in Joe Hayes' collection <u>The Day It Snowed Tortillas: Tales from Spanish New Mexico</u>. I have seen or heard versions of this same tale from French Canada and Tibet. This is the first folktale I ever told.

A Matter Between Friends: my version of an urban legend originally told to me in the early '80s by Bobby Haydocy. I published this tale as "The Blow-dried Cat" in a collection of stories

334

about the island of Clear Lake Shores, Texas. A similar version, titled "A Matter Between Friends," was included in the collection Best Stories from the Texas Storytelling Festival, edited by Finley Stewart.

CHAPTER 8
Discipline: Choices and Consequences

The Crane Wife: adapted from a traditional Japanese folktale. I have heard Jeannine Pasini-Beekman tell a beautiful version of this tale, which she adapted to the Texas Gulf Coast. This version was inspired by her telling.

The Gardener's Choice: a Jataka tale, attributed to Buddha. These tales were said to be delivered in northeast India between 563 and 483 BC, a true argument for the power and timelessness of a good story. I adapted a version titled "Responsibility" from the collection Jataka Tales, edited by Nancy DeRoin.

Not Our Problem: a traditional tale from Asia found in collections of Thai, Burmese, and Armenian folktales. A version appears in Margaret Read McDonald's Peace Tales: World Folktales to Talk About. This is a great story to use in any classroom.

Fear: one of my favorite Nasrudin tales. Storyteller Jim May shared this one with me. A short version can be found in The Exploits of the Incomparable Mulla Nasrudin, by Idries Shah. I collected a number of stories like this one during a year when fear became both my enemy and my ally.

Anger: again, a Nasrudin tale. See also The Subtleties of the Inimitable Mulla Nasrudin, also by Idries Shah.

Confusion: our friend Nasrudin once more (see Idries Shah, above). An ancient tradition of Nasrudin tales is sometimes observed that when one is told, six more must follow. It is handy to have storytellers Tom McDermott and Steve Kardaleff at the table if one is to follow this tradition.

CHAPTER 9
About Instruction: Knowing and Learning

Uncle Kenneth's Axe Handle: adapted from a Norwegian tale found in the collections of Peter Asbjornsen titled "Good Day, Fellow! Axe Handle." This entire chapter took shape after an Internet conversation I had with Sunwolf on what we know about knowing and learning.

The Sky Is Falling: never would I have imagined a version of Chicken Little being told from Pete's front steps.

The Blind Dixie Gospel Quartet Meets the King of the Circus: an adaptation of an ancient India tale of the Blind Men and the Elephant. I found a version in the 101 Tales of Wisdom ("Four Blind Men See an Elephant"), a regular text used by the Hindu followers of His Divine Holiness, Pramukh Swami Maharaj. The 101 tales are often used during the daily family meetings of his faithful. His Divine Holiness is a firm believer in the power of stories to teach and to guide.

Turtle Learns to Fly: a porqua story (why? story) told in many cultures. I have heard Native American tellers Gayle Ross and Joe Bruchac tell different versions. "How Turtle Flew South for the Winter" is in Bruchac's and Michael Caduto's Keepers of the Earth collection. "Bye-Bye," a Haitian version, appears in Diane Wolkstein's The Magic Orange Tree.

Wisdom or Air? a version of this Brazilian folktale titled "The First Lesson" can be found in Pleasant DeSpain's Thirty-Three Multicultural Tales to Tell.

Joey Meets the Board of Education: an original tale that has several qualities of the story framework found in the culture of poverty. It is my attempt at allowing Carlos to play the role of teller.

EPILOGUE
Story Roots

The Perfect Shot: a traditional Jewish folktale that I heard told by Rabbi Jimmy Kessler; it can be found on the audiotape A Storytelling Treasury: Tales Told at the 20th Anniversary National Storytelling Festival, by California storyteller Steve Sanfield, titled "A Bull's-Eye Every Time."

RESOURCES

Books:

Afro-American Folk Tales: Stories from the Black Tradition, edited and selected by Roger D. Abrahams. Pantheon Books. New York, NY. 1985.

Norwegian Folktales, collected by Peter Asbjornsen. Pantheon Books. New York, NY. 1982.

Keepers of the Earth, by Michael Caduto and Joseph Bruchac. Fulcrum Publishing. Golden, CO. 1988, 1989.

The Jack Tales, collected by Richard Chase. Houghton-Mifflin Co. New York, NY. 1943.

The Tiger's Whisker and Other Tales from Asia and the Pacific, collected by Harold Courlander. Henry Holt & Co. New York, NY. 1995.

Putting the World in a Nutshell: The Art of the Formula Tale, by Sheila Dailey. H.W. Wilson. New York, NY. 1994.

Jataka Tales, edited by Nancy DeRoin. Houghton-Mifflin Co. Boston, MA. 1975.

Thirty-Three Multicultural Tales to Tell, collected by Pleasant DeSpain. August House, Inc. Little Rock, AR. 1993.

Stories of the Spirit, Stories of the Heart, edited by
Christina Feldman and Jack Kornfield.
HarperCollins. New York, NY. 1991.

The Day It Snowed Tortillas: Tales from Spanish
New Mexico, collected by Joe Hayes. Mariposa
Publishing. Santa Fe, NM. 1982.

Peace Tales: World Folktales to Talk About, compiled by Margaret Read McDonald. The Shoe
String Press. Hamden, CT. 1992.

Best Loved Stories Told at the National Storytelling
Festival, selected by NAPPS. National
Storytelling Press. Jonesborough, TN. 1991.

More Best Loved Stories Told at the National
Storytelling Festival, selected by NAPPS. National Storytelling Press. Jonesborough, TN.
1992.

101 Tales of Wisdom, as told by His Divine Holiness, Pramukh Swami Maharaj.
Swaminarayan Aksharpith. Gujarat, India.
1996.

Zen Flesh, Zen Bones, compiled by Paul Reps. Anchor Books, Doubleday. New York, NY. 1989.

The Exploits of the Incomparable Mulla Nasrudin,
by Idries Shah. Octagon Press. London, En-
gland, UK. 1983.